CHRONICLES
OF THE
SECOND REALM

BROTHERHOOD OF EXORCISTS

CHRONICLES OF THE SECOND REALM

BROTHERHOOD OF EXORCISTS

CURTIS REID EDGETT

Clovercroft Publishing

Chronicles of the Second Realm

©2016 by Reid Edgett

Published by Clovercroft Publishing, Franklin, Tennessee

Published in association with Larry Carpenter of Christian Book Services, LLC of Franklin, Tennessee

Edited by Christy Callahan

Cover Design and Interior Layout Design by Suzanne Lawing

ISBN: 978-1-942557-53-1

Printed in the United States of America

I would like to dedicate this book to my loving wife. With all the frustration we went through with my spelling and grammar, I want you to know that I appreciate every moment that you spent working on the book. Tub I tsum od gnihtemos lufyalp sjut ot yonna uoy. Ha ha ha.

Acknowledgements

I'd like to thank my parents, Curt and Cindy Edgett, for always encouraging me to follow my dreams even when it got difficult. I love you both, and I appreciate everything you have done for me.

Also, I'd like to thank my best friend, Christian McDonald, for giving me great ideas for my characters. Without you in my life, I wouldn't have been able to come up with some of my characters' personalities, like a loud-mouthed, spastic Tyler.

A special thank-you to everyone who read this book and gave me constructive feedback: Debbie Mengloi, Connor Brock, Traci Cory, and Andrea Arnold.

And finally, to my brothers, Brandon and Keith, and my sister, Thayse; you guys really didn't do anything, but I thought I'd mention you anyways.

"THE TRUE SIGN OF INTELLIGENCE IS NOT KNOWLEDGE BUT IMAGINATION."

—ALBERT EINSTEIN

Prologue

Ba-dum. Ba-dum. Ba-dum. Ba-dum. The sound of a fading heartbeat, another soul about to leave this earth. In the middle of a dimly lit sidewalk in Edgefield, South Carolina, was a body sprawled out on the sidewalk. A man's face was lying on its side against the cold, hard pavement. His body was unable to move. Air was no longer reaching his lungs, and he began gasping for air. He didn't look a day over twenty-five. He had a well-built body and thick, black hair and was dressed in a blue button-down shirt, black slacks, and dress shoes. The three bullet holes in his back were pulsing with blood that dripped down his sides. A crimson pool surrounded his body.

"Hee-hee!" The child giggled. "Higher, Daddy! Higher!"

Earlier that day the man was pushing his son on the swings at the local park. The park just so happened to be right across the street from his work place. His wife and son would often visit him while he was on lunch break, affording them time together in the middle of the day. When he got home, his wife asked him to run and get some groceries from the store right down the block. Before he left to run the errand, he went upstairs to say good night to his son.

He walked into the room to find his son with the bed sheets pulled up tight to his face with eyes just peeking over.

"Daddy, I saw a monster under my bed!" the boy exclaimed.

He checked under the bed, for his son's peace of mind, only to find nothing there. "I must have scared it," the man said to his son, "but I'll make sure he never comes back."

He picked up a teddy bear and handed it to his son. "This is Mr. Fluffanutter; he's here to protect you. If you ever get scared, just hug Mr. Fluffanutter really tight and he'll get rid of the monsters. OK?"

"Uh-huh," the boy responded.

"Good night, son."

The man kissed his son on the head, walked out, and closed the door behind him. He headed out the front door of the apartment building and down the street to the local convenience store. They lived in a small town where the crime was almost nonexistent and the people were average, middle-class Americans. To have someone caught up in a drive-by shooting was unheard of in Edgefield, South Carolina. The news reported that the intended target of the shooting was a teenage male who had recently left his gang and made off with huge amounts of drug money. A couple of members from the gang had been searching for him and finally found him. They tailed him to the local convenience store around nine o'clock at night and waited for him. He walked out of the store, Yoohoo in hand, without knowing that he was being followed.

There was another man exiting the very same convenience store, his hands full of groceries, walking in the same direction as the teen. A Jeep rolled up alongside the man, just out of sight of the kid. Guns were raised and pointed at the teenager. Without a second thought, the man behind him dropped his bags and rushed up to the boy. He shoved the kid down a narrow alleyway as bullets began to fly. However, in an attempt to rescue the kid, the Good Samaritan got caught in the crossfire. A few moments later, the shop clerk ran out and started popping off shotgun rounds at the Jeep. The Jeep sped off and out of range.

The victim of this unfortunate series of events was pronounced dead upon arrival. He was identified as Michael Adler. He was twenty-seven years old. He was survived by his wife, Lauren, and Owen, his five-year-old son. Now, the actual target of this attack managed to get away; but the car was later identified, and the attackers were apprehended by the Edgefield Police Department.

Chapter One

I was walking down the hallway, on the way to English class, lockers to the left and right. The other kids were making their way to class. You would think that the bright-yellow lockers, the nauseatingly bright-green walls, and wide-open area brimming with colorful plants would bring a sense of joy to everyone's face who inhabited this stinkhole—but not really. Every kid looked just as dismal as the others around them. And the teachers here were kidding everyone, including themselves, that following your dreams and having hope for the future is possible. Most of the student body was stressed, trying to decide what they wanted to do with their future. Plans were being made, college acceptances were coming in, and I was just there. I merely existed.

I had been working at the local hardware store since I was fourteen. I had no plans for the future, no friends, no girlfriend; even my own family thought I was a freak. At least I had a 'reason' for all of this. When I was younger, I thought

I saw a monster in my room. It was a shadowy creature with a menacing appearance. My parents thought I just had an overactive imagination, but I kept seeing things like this. My parents finally had enough and they took me to a psychiatrist, and I was diagnosed with schizophrenia. The doctor prescribed medication. Then, the visions started to go away. When the other parents found out about my disorder, most of them wouldn't let their kids play with me.

In middle school, not much had changed; I was the weird kid who sat in the back. I was by myself a lot, but I did OK. I did my assignments and projects on time and never called attention to myself. The closest that I had ever gotten to having a friend was when I met this girl, Emiko. She was only a little shorter than I was, with shoulder-length, jet-black hair and a nice smile. She was the only kid that ever talked to me. She came in midsemester and was only there for a couple of weeks. Her dad was a wealthy businessman; and her family was always traveling. I hadn't seen her since then. The last day that I talked to her, she was talking about Christianity and how God is all around.

She said, "God is everywhere. He watches over us and protects us. It doesn't matter that you do bad things. He still loves you."

I didn't really understand what she was talking about at the time. I just thought that God dwelled in churches and only cared if you followed the rules of the church and stuff. I didn't really give it much thought.

Once I got to high school, you'd think people would mature, and that I would have made more friends. Nope. I was a senior in high school and things had stayed pretty much the same; except I had the highest ranking you can get on all first-person shooter games. There I was: six foot one, eighteen years old, sitting in my school gym eating lunch.

The gym was dimly lit, with only a few large hanging light

fixtures. I had my smartphone out listening to one of my favorite hardcore bands. No one was in the gym; it was just me—alone—again. I tried sitting in the lunchroom a couple of times, but no matter who was sitting around me, food always found a way to hit me. And the last time I was in there, one of the jocks thought that it would be funny to shoot peas through a straw from ten feet away, with me as the target.

I was getting tired of the abuse, so I calmly picked up some of the peas and put them on my food tray. I got up with my tray and walked over to him. "I think you dropped some of your peas."

The guy had blonde, spiked hair, brown eyes, and earrings. He was wearing a golden football shirt, some dark-blue jeans, and flip-flops. "No, I didn't." He looked around the table at his friends and laughed.

"Yes, you did, and I think you should have them back." As I said that, I used my cafeteria tray like a baseball bat and smashed him across the face. As I made contact, the tray bent and broke in half under the force. The dude's body fell out of the chair and hit the concrete floor.

I found out later that I fractured his nose. I was somewhat disappointed that I didn't fully break it off or anything. At least no one messed with me after that. So I decided it was best for me to find somewhere secluded to eat lunch; and the gym, so far, had been the best choice.

As I was sitting on the bleachers, a finger reached for my left earbud. I felt a sudden tap on my headphones. I looked up and no one was around. The atmosphere felt heavy. I took my headphones out and searched for what caused this feeling. I saw nothing but dark shadows in parts of the room.

After lunch, I headed back to class. I sat down at my uncomfortable, hard plastic desk and put my head down with my arms folded. The teacher ignored me and went on with her teaching for the last class. I started to drift off to sleep when I heard a voice that whispered, "Are you ready to die yet?" I was jolted awake and yelled a little bit. The whole class turned and looked at me.

The teacher stared at me and said very sarcastically, "I'm sorry, did I wake you?"

"No ma'am, I would never sleep in your class," I very smartly said to Mrs. Mahler.

The class chuckled a little. She looked away and continued with the class, pretending I didn't say anything. I couldn't get over the voice. I felt like someone was inches away from my ear and whispering to me.

The bell rang; everyone collected their things and headed out the door. I made my way down the hall, through the courtyard to the other side of the school where the music room was located. My parents thought that I needed to do something productive and creative with my life, so they had forced me into the after-school arts program. I had a choice between drama, dance, or learning an instrument. I opted for one-on-one instruction with Mr. Bryans for guitar. He was a nice guy and very knowledgeable about music. He reminded me of the nerdy KFC guy. The white hair and beard made him look older than he really was though. I'd only been working with him for a few months, but I'd learned a lot of basic stuff. After that day's lesson was over, I grabbed my backpack and guitar and headed to the bus lane for the activities bus.

Oh, crap! Just then I realized I had left my lunch box in the gym. As I made my way through the lime-green hallways, I started to notice something. Around each corner of the walls, I saw shadows.

Maybe those stupid lamps are busted, I tried to reassure myself. The shadows seemed to move where and when I moved. As I took each step, I heard the movement grow nearer. It was like someone had closed a door; except every time that I looked over my shoulder, no one was there. *Whoosh!* I heard a small gust of what sounded like wind.

"What the hell are you?" I yelled.

There was no reply. I was only answered by the strange looks of the janitors and some of the kids waiting for the late bus.

The shadows began to fade.

"Thank God." I sighed in relief.

Then I began to hear something, like somebody sharpening a knife or the gnashing of teeth. It was a grating sound and it seemed to get louder and louder as I neared the final right turn into the gymnasium.

I approached the doors to the gym and they swung open with relative ease. The gym was empty and deserted. Unlike the rest of the school, at this hour, the gym was dark. The stadium lights were off, and the basketball hoops were put up for the night. I noticed my lunch box sitting on the bleachers. I walked towards the bleachers to retrieve it.

"Are you ready to die?"

I was just about to pick up my lunch box; my hands were almost wrapped around it. I felt a sudden surge of fear and absolute terror run up my spine. I barely managed to utter, "Huh?"

"Yes you, Owen."

I gulped.

"Nobody will miss you anyways. Everyone thinks you are crazy. What's the point of your pitiful and meaningless existence?"

"Excuse me?"

"But what would I know? I'm not even there."

"Yeah, you're not real." I pointed into the thin air in front of me.

"How about now?" I could hear the voice coming from right behind me. I could feel the creature breathing down my neck. I whip my whole body around to see nothing.

"You're not real!" I shouted.

"Oh, I am very real." The creature jumped out in front of me. Its fur was gray and matted, like it hadn't groomed itself in several weeks. It had fangs that were very large and yellow. It looked like a werewolf with a crazed look in its eyes. Its dingy fur was tinged crimson red, like blood near the tips. The creature had an odor about it, not like the cleaning products used in the gym—like a cesspool. The creature opened its mouth wider, exposing its teeth and further spreading the smell. "You can't escape me."

I fell to the ground and hunched over. "You aren't real. You aren't real. You aren't real!"

"I *am* real. But who is going to believe you? Everyone thinks you are crazy—and you are."

I finally managed to gather the strength to stand up, and eventually the blood flow came back to my legs. I decided to screw the idea of getting my lunch box and began to run. I made my way down the halls and around the corners.

"You cannot escape. You can never escape me."

"Shut up! Shut up! Shut...up!" I screamed. I began to run faster. I made it to one of the staircases and ran up them. I passed the first floor and then the second floor. I finally made it to the roof.

"You have nowhere to run and nowhere to hide. You are alone. Nobody cares about you. It would be best to just end it here."

I looked around. I noticed the edge of the roof of the school building. *He's right. If I survived this and told somebody, they would just say that I need to take my meds or that it's just my imagination. There is no point in dealing with this torment.*

"You might as well just end it," the creature eerily whispered. "Just jump."

I stood on the edge of the building. I looked just over the edge.

"Go on. Nobody will mourn you. All you are is a child, a messed-up, broken toy."

It's almost easy. It's easier than being all alone. I stood on that ledge for a moment. I began to pace and contemplate jumping.

The creature came back into my field of vision. The sight of it was just as frightening; and it continued to taunt me mercilessly.

I stepped up onto the ledge for what I had hoped would be the final time. *No more hurt, no more pain—it must be nice.* I reassured myself that this was the right and only possible decision. *And all I have to do is jump.* I had one foot on the ledge and I put one foot out in front, nothing keeping it safe, except my socks and my chucks. I closed my eyes and prepared to leap. Just as I started to lift my foot off the solid ground...

Whap!

Something hurled me into the wall near the staircase and knocked the wind out of me. I sat slightly concussed on the ground. I wasn't sure if what was happening was another hallucination or it was real. I saw a tall and rather muscular gentleman. He looked very composed and calm. His dark locks were gelled back very neatly; and he wore a black leather trench coat. I saw him grab a sword from the sheath he had on his back. His sword resembled Siegfried from Soul Caliber V's sword, Caladbolg. It was a very sizeable broadsword that definitely needed to be wielded with two hands and great strength; but this man moved it as if it were made of Styrofoam, and with ease.

The stranger walked towards me. I grew more and more puzzled with each movement. The man brought up his sword with the blade pointed in my direction. He held the handle of the sword with both hands. He raised the sword up and plunged it down quickly into my chest. My body let out two different screams. "Ah!" I felt no physical pain, but my chest burned like it was on fire. My body thrust upward, and all of my energy began to leave me. I couldn't keep my eyes open any longer; and then slowly, they started to close. The last thing I remember seeing was a dark, smoky figure rise from my body.

Chapter Two

My eyes flickered, for what felt like a very long time, open and close, open and close. Eventually, they stayed open and I made the decision to wake up. I felt a rhythmic, pulsating, and pounding sensation in my head.

Holy crap, I had the strangest dream, I thought, unsure if I should be relieved or totally freaked out. I put my hands on my head, as if I were trying to contain the pounding that was in my head.

"Jeez, what time is it?" I asked rhetorically. I looked over at my alarm clock and saw that it was about 3:28 in the morning. I let out a groan. I tried for about an hour to go back to sleep. I fell asleep until five. I gave up on the idea of sleeping, pulled out my Gameboy, and restarted my Pokémon yellow game. I played and even won a few badges in the span of an hour and a half. I was just about to battle Lieutenant Surge for my third badge when I heard the buzzing of my alarm clock. *Better get ready*, I sarcastically thought to myself.

I showered, got dressed, brushed my teeth, and then went downstairs. I saw my mom and Stan already in the kitchen. Stan had his mug of coffee in one hand and his phone in the other, probably looking at the local news. Mom was at the counter making me and my little sister's lunches for school. Gracie was eating her favorite cereal at the dining room table. As I walked down the stairs, both parents looked up at me.

"Hey bud, when did you get in last night?" Stan asked. "We didn't even hear you come in."

"I don't remember." I didn't even recall walking home or getting into my bed. *How did I get home?*

"How did guitar lessons go?" my mom asked.

"Good. I learned more chords and a new scale."

"Very cool," she said excitedly. "Soon you'll be rocking out and getting all the ladies."

I rolled my eyes and headed to the fridge. I opened it up and grabbed the carton of orange juice. There was only a quarter of it left, and I started to drink out of it.

My mom heard the gulping sounds and turned around to scold me. "Owen, don't drink from the carton. Grab a glass."

"But there's not much left."

"I don't care. You shouldn't do that anyways."

I started to drink more out of it while slowly backing away from her.

She gave me a dirty look. "Owen, put that down."

"Uh-uh," I said, with a mouth full of orange juice.

She grabbed a spatula from a jar on the kitchen counter and waved it at me. "Do I need to pat you on the butt like you're five?"

Gracie looked over and laughed with food still in her mouth. I raised my hands and surrendered with the carton in one hand, bottle cap in the other. I looked at the jug and determined that I could finish this in one more gulp. So I quickly downed the rest of it before she could say anything.

"Ah." I let out a sigh of accomplishment. I screwed the lid back on and tossed it at my mom. She caught it and looked at me with a smile and shook her head. "Hey Mom, we're out of orange juice," I said, walking toward her. I danced around her, grabbed my lunch, and started out the door. "Bye!" I shouted, heading out the door.

I heard everyone else yell back, "Bye! Have a good day!" I closed the door and made my way down the street to the bus stop. It was a day, just like any other. I found my seat on the bus and quickly disengaged from reality. I put in my headphones and entered into "All That Remains," quickly attracted by the melodic, yet hard sounds of the guitar instrumental and the driving beat of the drums. God, I enjoyed it so much! It was all so nice, just looking out the window, thinking about absolutely nothing and watching the buildings go by. Then we arrived at the school—back to reality.

I roamed the halls with contempt. I had my hands in the pockets of my faded, black jeans and the hood of my purple hoodie was up and covering my head. The bell rang. I went through my day. All the classes just kind of happened. I barely remembered the lessons from the day. It was all kind of a blur. My brain was consumed only by thoughts of last night's dream, and my notebook was filled with drawings of the creature-thing that attacked the mysterious, coiffed stranger and me.

I went through history, English IV, discrete math, and finally made it to Spanish class. I figured that I could sleep through that class, as there was a substitute teacher.

"Mrs. Videl just experienced the miracle that is childbirth, so I will be subbing this class," said the teacher, who sounded like she smoked twenty packs a day and looked like she got her hairstyle ideas from Marge Simpson. "Pull out your textbooks and appear busy," she continued as textbooks practically flew out from under the desks. "You can listen to your music, headphones, or whatever; you can make crude doodles—just look like you're trying or something."

I quickly followed orders, picking up my textbook and plugging into Green Day. I began to drum along with Tré Cool and decided to turn to the page where verb conjugation was discussed. I was pretending to be interested in how to conjugate verbs, when out of the corner of my eye, I saw him. I spotted him from a distance and he seemed to be waving at me. Weird.

This guy looked like the guy from my dream. He had donned the same black trench coat and even had the same coif. It was starting to freak me out. I could make out his muscular build and see his facial features. It was him. He was still waving. I put my face in the book and did my best to ignore him for the remaining ninety minutes of class.

The bell rang. And just like that, class was dismissed. As everybody dispersed and disappeared into either the car line or the bus loop, I heard the voice. It was calling my name. "Owen, Owen," the man cried out.

I turned around. He knew my name. I began to walk towards him.

"There you are, Owen," the man said as he got closer to me. His look of concern turned into a somewhat reassuring smile.

"I saw you l-last night," I stammered as I continued to fight the throbbing inside of my head. "Y-y-you were in m-my dream."

"That wasn't a dream; that was real."

I stared at him in disbelief. "I'm sorry. What?" I asked, dumbfounded.

He gazed back at me. "Yeah."

I couldn't understand how or why he was being so nonchalant about this. "So, I almost jumped off a building and you really plunged a sword into me?" I asked curiously.

He paused and appeared to be thinking about his answer.

"Uh-huh."

"Who are you anyway—and what happened last night?" I asked indignantly.

"Do you really want to know?" As he said this, the man reached into his pants pocket and pulled something out with a closed fist. He stretched out his hand with his palm facing upwards to reveal two pills, a red one and a blue one.

My eyes grew wide. "Are we in 'The Matrix'?"

The man slapped me on the back of the head. "No, these are for your headache."

I stood in amazement as this seemingly angelic man had just Gibb-smacked me.

"That probably didn't help though," he said, smirking all the while.

"Not really, no."

"It's time for business." His smirk quickly turned into a seriously straight face. "We have to go."

"What?" I said. "I still don't understand."

"Get in the car, kid." He hastily pushed me into his jet-black 2016 Camaro.

We drove off to 'only God knows where.' We then pulled up to a very swanky-looking office building. When the stranger and I walked in, it was clearly swanky on the inside, too. It had a modern interior with sitting areas spread throughout. The far back wall had a something hanging about twenty feet up. It was a giant medieval shield with a broadsword going down the center and angelic wings protruding from behind.

We walked up to a receptionist's desk. She looked not a day over twenty-five and was chewing gum while she was reading a newspaper. The stranger approached her desk. He said nothing and the receptionist quickly looked up over her newspaper. "Hi, Marth." Her face was beet red by this point.

Marth waved me over. The receptionist noticed me and the fact that I was with him. She stopped making googly eyes at

Marth and looked at me. "Hi, Owen. We've been expecting you."

I didn't know what to say, so I said nothing. I watched as it looked like Marth was signing us in at some kind of office.

"Fourth floor." The receptionist winked at him.

Marth turned and thanked the receptionist, and we boarded the elevator. We arrived on the fourth floor; Marth and I turned a corner and entered what looked like a theater.

"Class is about to start," Marth said.

"Class?"

"This will give you all the answers that you want. I'll come find you later. I'll be in the gym."

"Where's the gym?"

"I'll be back before the class ends," Marth said as the door closed.

I walked into the auditorium. It looked very grandiose and very expansive. There were ten other people inside scattered about.

A man walked up onto the stage to the podium. He introduced himself. "Good afternoon, students. My name is Professor Hutcheson. How is everyone's head doing, hmm?" He chuckled to himself. "Yes, yesterday really did happen. It was not a dream. And yes, you did see demons."

The other people in the room started looking around at each other with puzzled expressions on their faces.

"Demons are everywhere and they are messing with everyone and trying to destroy us. Why? Because we are made in God's image. The one who comes against us, Satan, hates God. So he and his demon pals hate us as well. But…we have dominion over them. God has gifted all of you with the ability to do battle against these demonic forces. He has empowered you to see these demons and destroy them.

"Demons can only enter a person's body by being allowed in. People don't literally say, 'Demons come in me.' No, they slowly creep in by things you say and do. It's all about guarding your heart. If you don't allow negative things into your life, you won't be prone to demonic activity. Each demon has a different job. Some are there to fuel your anger, some make you sick, and some just come to bring depression upon you. Demons have been doing this since the beginning of time; so they know all the different ways of deception and how to manipulate humans. They are very smart and they usually work in teams. One may be attacking while the other is distracting you.

"We break each demon into classifications based on size and intelligence. Class-one demons are the small, annoying ones that don't say anything. They just buzz around trying to distract you. Their size ranges from as small as a mouse to the size of a river otter. Class-two demons are slightly bigger; their average size is like a full-grown cow. They can't talk, but they can roar, shriek, and make many high-pitch screams. The class-three demons are usually four-to-fourteen-feet tall. They vary in shape and features. These can communicate with people in any language. They know how to terrify and destroy people's hopes and dreams; so be cautious when fighting them. The only class-four demon is Satan, but he doesn't come off his underworld throne for anything. I guess he has to save all his energy for Armageddon.

"Now, how do you exorcise a demon, you may ask? There are many different ways. As exorcists, we have many types of abilities that we can use. Most exorcists use weapons, like swords, staffs, daggers, battle-axes, war hammers, and things of that nature. Soon you will see you natural abilities start to increase: speed, strength, reflexes. You'll be able to do things that normal human beings can only dream of. There are some skills that have not been documented that are still within our abilities. Let your imagination run wild and create your own style. Also, your weapons can't be seen by ordinary people.

So when you pull them out, you'll just look crazy. Try to keep your battles out of the public view."

He took a slight pause.

"When? When is very important. When can we exorcise a demon? When they try to manifest or take over a human host. Demons are around everyone all the time whispering in their ears to do this or do that. They're trying to make bad things seem harmless or normal. They love using people of influence. Actors, actresses, models, bands, artists, and politicians—they help set the normal. So when they take over a human, that is our chance. Until then, there is nothing we can do."

"Why can't we destroy them on sight?" some guy in the room shouted out.

"Great question!" the professor said. "The answer is free will. Humans have free will to do whatever they want; but once they are taken over by a demon, they lose their free will and are now being controlled by the demon. This allows us to take action and destroy them. But *not* until they manifest. And finally, why? Why you, you may ask? Because, He loves to use the least likely or the last picked. He did not pick you at random. He chose you because you are special and you will make an impact in your area or more. And because he chose you, His light will shine the brightest when you achieve success. Now, I know this is a lot to take in. You can go back to you regular lives and give up this gift and you'll never see anything like this again. But this war is going on whether or not you join the fight. It's your choice. That's all I have for you. You are dismissed."

The doors on both sides of the auditorium started to open and the professor made his way off the stage. People started to get up and make their way out. I exited the auditorium and saw Marth waiting for me outside the doors.

"So Owen, would you like to learn how to be an exorcist?"

I paused for a moment. "Sure, why not." I shrugged my

shoulders. "My mom always says I need to challenge myself. And what's more challenging than taking on the forces of darkness led by Satan himself?"

Marth and I both smiled.

"When do we start?" I asked.

"Now," Marth replied.

CHAPTER THREE

Marth and I meandered down the hallways back towards the elevators. We hopped in and Marth pushed the button that should take us to the basement. The giant, metallic doors closed shut and the elevator music began, as did our descent. We arrived in the basement. It looked like an abandoned airplane hangar. It had a dirty concrete floor, and the faded-red support beams were visible. As we walked out of the elevator, Marth turned to the right and there was a control panel. It had a palm scanner, and Marth laid his hand on the screen. The board lit up and it sounded like turbines starting up.

Immediately, the tables and lockers rose from beneath the floor. The lockers formed an L shape with a table and bench seats in the midst of them. The lockers each had a variety of weapons. In each locker, there was a different category of armament. In one locker, there were different kinds of daggers—in another an abundance of arrows and bows. There was a multitude of swords, hammers, axes, and other dangerous tools.

"OK, Owen, today we're going to be working with weapons," Marth began. "Pick out the weapon that you will feel the most comfortable with."

I scanned the room and I felt like a kid in a candy store. I walked up to all of the lockers and examined the weapons that they contained. I especially liked the hammers, so I grabbed the biggest one I could find. I proudly showed Marth my choice. Marth looked back at me with a very surprised and seemingly confused, yet snarky look on his face.

"Pick that up," Marth commanded.

I tried to pick up the hammer, and by try, I mean failed at trying. The head of the hammer was two feet wide and as tall as me.

Marth noticed my struggle, came over, and picked up the hammer effortlessly. "It's as light as a feather." He stifled his laughter. "Your abilities are limited by the human thought process. You thought that it was going to be super heavy, and in turn, it was. It is what you make it. It's as light as a feather."

Marth finished his sentence and then proceeded to flip the hammer on his finger, all with ease, not breaking a sweat, even though it looked as if it weighed a ton. Marth tossed the hammer to me.

In my head, I was chanting, *Light as a feather, light as a feather, light as a fe— Oh, I caught it.*

Marth walked back over to the control panel and began pressing buttons. The screen lit up. "All right," he said. "Time to test it out."

Targets began to come down from the ceiling. They hung like chandeliers, but they definitely were meant to be hit. They were shaped like stone pumpkins. I gripped my hammer tightly and began to swing. I was hitting targets, one right after the other. The fragments of each target crumbled when you hit the ground. The hammer was a very interesting weapon to hold. It started to feel a little tiring, so I thought about switching weapons. I walked back over to the lockers.

"Done already?" Marth asked.

"No, I'm just gonna try something else."

I examined my newly acquired arsenal once again. Then, one of the swords in the cabinets caught my eye. Its style was like a traditional Japanese katana. It had a slightly blue-tinged metal blade and was very sleek. The handle had a very good grip. I slung the sheath over my back and pulled it out. I went back out to the course and began to experiment with it a little. I sliced through targets, right and left. Then, Marth pushed a few more buttons on the control panel. I soon saw much bigger 'targets' appear. They were humanoid in shape and looked as if they were made of stone. They looked like bulky stone muscle men. Marth kept pushing more buttons. The 'targets' began to come at me and were ready for attack. They marched after me and began to chase me. Expletives were running through my head, all of which were directed towards Marth. I lifted my sword and began to fight.

Cling. I could hear my sword go through the stone. I swung up at an angle to slice one directly in front of me, then spun around and slashed downward to another one coming from the right. I could hear a crash as the pieces of stone fell to the ground with each swing of my sword. I felt like a tornado of destruction. I realized, after fighting the first one, that this wasn't impossible and that the only limits here were the limits that I placed on myself. As I continued to slice through the sentinels, they would fall before me. All the sentinels were smashed into rubble on the ground all around me. I stood there panting for a second, and then I heard clapping. Marth was clapping, a golf clap, but applause nonetheless. Marth pressed a few more buttons and little robots came out onto the course and started removing the rubble. The remains of the fallen sentinels were quickly wiped away, like the remaining bowling pins at a bowling alley.

I walked back over to Marth.

"Have you chosen your weapon?" he asked.

"Yeah."

"Good. Then it's yours." He snidely smiled. "Moving on." Marth walked over to the control booth, very nonchalantly, and pressed a button on the pad. "Let him in."

I could hear a door creak open. It came from a small side door, on the left in the middle of the structure. A man emerged, looking to be forty-ish and of Asian descent. As he got closer to us, Marth pulled out a chair from behind the control panel and put it in the middle of the room. The man walked towards the chair. Marth interjected, "Haru, this is Owen. Owen—Haru."

We shook hands. "Haru is the owner and executive chef at my favorite Asian fusion restaurant," Marth continued. "He has been struggling with demon possession; and Mr. Haru here has volunteered to have us exorcise this demon."

"What?" I was flipping my ish right then. "Now?"

"Yeah, you just practiced with your sword. Don't you want to try it out on an actual demon?" Marth asked, slightly amused.

"Um." I looked around the room nervously, mentally un-prepared for such a task.

"The best way to learn is hands-on experience," Marth said, very cheerfully. His smile was so big; it looked like it hurt.

I sighed a sigh of defeat. "Fine."

Meanwhile, Haru had already sat down in the chair and was waiting patiently. Marth walked over to Haru and began to reassure him. "OK, Haru, this should be quick and painless. The only thing that you will experience is maybe blacking out for a few minutes."

"OK." Haru nodded his head.

"Wait, wait, wait, I thought we couldn't exorcise demons

until they manifest," I questioned.

"You're right, but if the person knows about this demon and it has already manifested multiple times, the person can give us consent to exorcise the demon that is hindering them," Marth explained.

"OK." Marth looked to me. "We are going to begin."

I looked at Haru and took in a big gulp of air. Marth stood in front of Haru and began to lift his hands. He mumbled something to himself, and then his hands burst into flames. But it looked like a controlled burn, because the fire never left his palms. He reached into Haru through his chest and tugged on something. This something didn't look like it wanted to leave Haru's body. But Marth insisted that it did, and pulled harder. And eventually, he pulled it halfway out. The top half of a pale-gray, stony-looking Cyclops stuck out of Haru's body. It roared and displayed its brute strength by tugging back against Marth; but Marth gave it one last grab, ripped it out, and threw it back behind him. It was about fifteen feet tall and it looked to be the size of a dump truck. Haru was still in the chair; he looked limp and lifeless. The Cyclops laid against the wall of the warehouse. It looked like it was trying to gather its strength. Marth gestured to me, summoning me. I walked over towards Marth and the Cyclops, holding my sword in my hands and shaking all the while. I looked at the demonic figure as it lay before me; and I was scared. I lifted up my sword and prepared to plunge it into the demon's chest.

The demon's eye opened and I heard a thump of its foot and a whap. Its fight-or-flight response must have activated. The demon used its might and mountainous leg to kick me twenty feet from where I stood. I felt my flesh slam into the concrete wall. I peeled myself off the wall and stood up unharmed.

"Did you feel any pain?" Marth yelled over the giant's writhing about.

I looked myself over and saw no bruise or blemish, much

to my surprise. "No," I responded, still kind of surprised.

"Demons can't hurt us in the natural," Marth said. "Once they leave their human hosts, they are easier to kill; however, if they manage to take over a human body completely, they can cause some real damage."

I got back up with a renewed sense of confidence.

Marth finished with one last sentence. "Every demon has a weak spot; the main ones are the head, the tail, and the heart."

"Hmm." I charged at the demon with my sword over my head like I was ready for a fastball down home plate. I got about five feet away and jumped. My feet left the ground with unknown lightness. I soared ten feet in the air, eye level with the beast. It raised its hands and swatted me down. I plummeted back down to the ground and landed on my feet gently. I knew this was game on.

The demon let out a garbled roar. "Ah!"

This just got serious.

He rushed at me with his fists, swinging them wildly. When his fists hit the ground, I was surprised they didn't crack the concrete. I dodged each attack gracefully, not knowing how I was doing this. After the fifth punch, I'd had enough. When his fist hit the concrete, I swung my sword as hard as I could at his right arm. *Shing!* My sword sliced through his arm and it dropped to the floor with a thud.

The demon let out another roar. "Ah!" His arm started to smoke. It took about five seconds for it to evaporate into thin air. No blood was spilled anywhere; only smoke radiated from the wound. The demon looked and me. "You'll die for this, human!"

"Oh, my gosh, he talked!" I said to myself.

He raised his other arm and swung it down at me. I jumped sideways into a handspring to avoid the attack. I never knew I could move with this much agility and speed.

"OK, big boy, you're going down." I threw my sword up

over his head, almost touching the ceiling. Then, I ran at him with super speed and leapt up into the air. I lifted my legs up and thrust my heels into his chest. The demon started to fall as my sword did likewise. I rode the creature down to the ground like a wave.

When he hit the ground, I reached up and my sword landed perfectly in my hand. With my final slash, I lobbed the demon's head clean off. Smoke came pouring out of it and it completely disintegrated. I started breathing heavily.

"Nice work, Owen!" Marth said.

"Thanks." I was still trying to catch my breath.

Marth started walking over to Haru. "After each demon you destroy, you have to replace it with a seed."

"Huh?" I replied.

"Each demon represents something. To make sure that they can never return, we replace it with the opposite. For instance, this demon you just fought represented anger. So we will sow a seed of peace."

Marth stood in front of Haru and waved me over. After an awkward twenty-foot walk to him, Marth lifted his hands to the middle of Haru's body once again. As he did so, a seed appeared, floating in his right hand. It looked like a larger version of an almond but with a slight tinge of gold and a metallic luster. I put my sword back in its sheath and continued to watch. He pressed it against Haru's chest. His body seemed to absorb it. As it went in, it started to grow instantly. I could see inside his chest somehow; and I saw the seed begin to bloom into a flower. It reminded me of a lily. Haru slowly began to open his eyes.

"How do you feel?" Marth asked.

Haru looked around and let out a pleasant sigh. "Peaceful."

Marth and I looked at each other and smiled.

Haru stood up from the chair and stretched his arms. "I'm good."

"Good," Marth said cheerfully.

We started walking towards the door from which Haru originally entered, and then walked into a waiting room of sorts. The room was almost entirely white except for the accent wall, which was a bright lime green. The white walls were decorated with a few pieces of art, bringing splashes of color into the room. There was a bright-orange desk that looked like it came right out of *The Jetsons*, except there was no receptionist. To my left was a big, circular mirror. When I looked at myself, I saw that the sword on my back was gone. I panicked. I reached back for it and could still feel the hilt.

Strange...

I blew it off and continued to follow Marth and Haru down the hall. When we finally turned the corner, an excited family greeted us. There were hugs exchanged between Haru and a woman, whom I'm guessing was his wife. She had long, jet-black hair and wore a very frilly, pink top, a black skirt, and flat-soled shoes.

His two children, a boy and a girl, attacked him with bear hugs. The boy appeared older; his dark hair was slicked back and he wore a long-sleeved shirt, some cargo pants, and sneakers. The girl had short, black hair and wore black flats and a purple, flowered dress.

As Haru and his wife exchanged embraces, they were also exchanging words with each other in Japanese. They looked at each other happily, both of them smiling.

Then Haru's wife turned to Marth and started speaking some words in Japanese. Marth replied back in Japanese. Tears began to well up in her eyes, and Marth comforted her with a warm hug. Then Haru approached me and put out his hand. I shook his hand, and he smiled at me and said, "Thank you." Haru then went over to Marth and shook his hand. The family left, seemingly more together and peaceful than they were before.

Marth looked over at me. "This is why I love my job. When I can help families, it gives me a sense of fulfillment in life."

We walked over to the elevators, pressed the button, and waited for one of them to come down. Marth and I got on. The elevator rose slowly to the main level where we got off. We walked back to the reception area to sign back out. The lady who greeted us when we entered was still there. She looked up at me. "So…did you enjoy yourself today?"

I wasn't quite sure what to say to such a simple question. "I'll let you know after I process everything," I replied, kind of sarcastically. I signed my name on the sign-out sheet.

"We'll see you two soon. Bye-bye now," the receptionist said, as we started toward the front door.

"Need a ride, Owen?"

"Sure."

We headed to Marth's car. We got in, buckled our seatbelts, and drove off. From the HQ to my house, it took about ten minutes. So Marth decided to fill the silence with questions about me.

"So Owen, tell me a little about yourself."

"Like what?"

"You know, when you were born, family, hobbies, sports, interests—stuff like that."

"Well, I was born here on July 5, 1996. I haven't left the state once. I really don't have that many hobbies; I just picked up the guitar."

"That's pretty cool…uh-huh."

"I don't have any sports teams that I root for. As for family, my dad was killed when I was young; and I barely remember him." I paused for a second. "My mom got remarried to Stan about eight years ago, and a year later they had Gracie. She's seven now and wants to be a ballerina just like all the girls her age."

"So, what about you?" I quickly said before he started asking more questions. "What's your story?"

"Well, um, I've never been married," he began. "Um…before I turned nineteen, I was in the navy; I served for a couple of years. I learned a lot of combat training. Once I got out of the navy, I was about twenty-two. I was invited to the Brotherhood of Exorcists," he continued. "I've done things that I'm not proud of. I was a runaway. I've never really had a home. I have two brothers. I am the youngest and always had to fight for attention from my family. Once I turned sixteen, I did things that I didn't want to do—"

We pulled up to my house before he got to finish.

"I guess I'll finish some other time," he said. "Tomorrow, we're going for a ride." He paused. "Well, sort of like a patrol, I guess. I'll show you the ropes on what we do in this town and how we can help. Are you available?"

"I-I'll let you know," I said hesitantly. I gave Marth my number and he gave me his card. I got out of the car, and all I could say was, "Thanks."

I walked up the stoop and up to my front door. I entered the living room and walked into the kitchen, where I saw Stan. He was still in his work attire with the exception of an apron. I saw him chopping up cucumbers. He looked at me. "Hey, Owen, where have you been?"

I experienced a brief moment of panic, and all I could muster was, "I-I w-was hanging out…with a new friend."

"Oh cool, you made a friend. That's really good. What did you guys do?" His curiosity must have been piqued.

"Um…we slayed demons…in this new video game, I guess." I stuck my hands in my pockets. "Yeah, something like that."

"Cool." He looked very satisfied either with my answer or the fact that I had made any sort of attempt at befriending someone. "Your mom will be home any minute." He pointed his knife at the cucumber that he was slicing. "Dinner is at seven sharp."

"OK."

I trudged up the stairs to my room. I face-planted onto my bed and lifted up my head. I got back up and decided to pick up my guitar and play the few chords that I knew. I repeated progressions like E minor, C, G, and D. I did this for a while and then drifted off to sleep.

CHAPTER FOUR

I tossed and turned through the night. It was the morning after, and I was still wearing the same clothes that I wore the day before. *Dang! So today is…Saturday. I don't have to work and I can just sleep.* I was trying to fall back asleep. I closed my eyes, but I didn't have a peaceful dream like I wanted. Instead, I was having this vision of the depths of hell. There were demons coming up to earth through the cracks in a sidewalk. They began to slay people right and left. Then eventually, they were in my house. They began to creep towards Gracie's room, with what I could only imagine were bad intentions—intentions to kill. I woke up and sat straight up in my bed with the sheet only covering part of my legs and feet. I woke up in a panic. I was sweating and hyperventilating. In and out, in and out, I breathed.

"Oh," I said, "it was only a dream."

I sat back in my bed and sighed a sigh of relief. I was now, fortunately and unfortunately, definitely awake. I sat on the edge of my bed and let my feet dangle for a minute, catching my breath. I got up, walked over to my bathroom, and turned on the faucet. I cupped my hands as the lukewarm water fell into them and splashed some on my face. I let out another sigh of relief. I walked out of my bathroom and headed back to my room, only to notice that there was a plate of food on my nightstand, possibly from last night. It was Stan's famous chicken potpie. There was a fork next to the plate and a sticky note next to it saying:

Just in case you want a midnight snack :)
—Stan

I placed the note back on the nightstand and smirked. I sat on my bed and ate the slice of pie. Even a little cold, it was still very good; I thoroughly enjoyed every morsel of it.

I threw on my blue jeans, a white skate shirt, and a hoodie. I walked around the house. It was ten o'clock. Mom and Stan had already left for work; and I guess Mom dropped Gracie off at dance class. I supposed that I had the house to myself.

Ding-ding.

I reached in my pants pocket and retrieved my phone. It was a text from Marth. It read, "I'm outside." I looked at it. Feeling perplexed, I opened the door to go outside and there was Marth leaning against his car. I asked Marth half-heartedly, "Where are we going?"

"We're going to go for a ride," he answered. "I'm going to show you the ropes of how to protect the city so you can do it on your own."

We got in the car and drove for a little while. We were driving through the downtown area; it was a very small town. There were lots of brick buildings, small shops, and four-way stops. As we were driving, Marth was explaining exactly what it is that we do. "I'm going to tell you what we do to protect the town. We just monitor outward manifestations of demonic activity."

"Uh…OK."

"Basically, when people start wigging out in public, any demonic presence that shows itself, tries to take over a human host, we're there to stop it," Marth continued. "That's kind of how I found you." He paused and took a breath. "We're sort of an underground operation. People can't always see demonic activity; but when the demons take over a human host, other humans can see it. However, they can't see the demonic presence; they just think the person under demonic influence is acting funny. People tend to be afraid of what they can't understand, so we try to keep it on the down low. We have a heightened sense of being able to detect a demonic presence. There are demonic presences everywhere; but we just investigate the outward manifestations. Demons are here. There's no getting rid of them completely; but we're here to take them out when they show themselves."

When he was finished speaking, the car stopped at a four-way stop. I looked to the left and to the right. To the right of us, there was a café. I guess Marth saw it, too. He turned into the parking lot and parallel parked the car. He turned the car off, took the key out of the ignition, and turned to me. "Hey, Owen, do you sense anything?"

I tried to quiet my many racing thoughts. "Kind of. I feel like there is something wrong with my heart and head at the same time."

Marth looked at me. "That's what we call the sixth sense. We are human, but we have been gifted with supernatural abilities."

"Well, what is it?"

Marth kept looking at me. "Oh, you know, a demon." He quickly and very nonchalantly opened the car door and left me.

Huh?

We walked towards the Blue Droplet Café. The building had many nice glass windows that peered into the spacey-style decor. Marth opened the double doors and I followed. There was a nice counter space in the very front right at the window where one could sit on the barstools and enjoy the quite minimal traffic.

We entered the building and heard someone yelling. The establishment was nice looking with its modern décor and wide array of colors. There was a guy at the counter shouting at the cashier. He was balding, on the large side, and wearing a trench coat over some jeans. He angrily wielded his fresh, hot coffee as he berated the poor barista. When I looked at him, I could literally see a demon behind the cashier. It was whipping her. The whip was slashing the girl on the back and behind the head. This guy had her on the verge of tears. I reached behind my back for a sword, but I was interrupted when Marth grabbed my arm. "Let's have a seat over in the corner."

We went to a secluded part of the café near the back and sat at another bar area overlooking the drive-thru Wendy's on the other side.

"Let's just observe for a second," Marth said casually.

I looked around as if I were sitting on pins and needles, very anxiously.

Marth cautioned, "We have to be very wise about our timing." He took one look towards the girl and the demon looked back at us.

The demon noticed us. I began to panic. Fight or flight set in. The demon looked a little afraid. He wrapped the whip around the girl's throat and started pulling her out. The girl, at this point, was starting to cry. On the other hand, the guy that was complaining about the coffee was saying things like, "You're useless. Where is your manager?"

The girl was just pleading, begging with her eyes, for him to stop. "I'm sorry, sir," she managed to say through her tears. "My manager is out right now, but he'll be right back."

"Well, you're an incompetent, stupid little girl! You don't even know how to make a cup of coffee!" he roared back at her.

Now sobbing, the girl could only apologize to the man about her questionable customer service. "I'm sorry. I'm so sorry...I can't take this!" the girl finally cried out. She took off her black cap in a huff then yanked off her apron and ran out the back door.

Marth looked at me as I stared at the situation like a deer in headlights. "Well, which one do you want to take?"

"What?" I asked, very dumbfounded, coming back to reality.

"Which one do you want to take?" he asked again.

I looked around again. "I only see one."

Marth pointed out the demon on the angry guy. It looked like a large, porcupine-esque creature; and it was puking on the man.

I took one glimpse at it, slightly grossed out. "Dibs on the chick!" I began to run out through the front door, chasing after the girl. I disregarded all obstacles in my way.

Marth looked at the demon possessing the guy and then back to me and just shrugged his shoulders. "I guess I got you," he said about the rather gnarly-looking demon attacking the man. Even in the midst of danger, he was still unfazed.

I ran around to the very back of the café. There was a fenced-in, L-shaped walkway near the back door. Not very far away, there was a Dumpster. I spotted the girl, and she was crying. I walked cautiously towards her and pulled out my sword. I shouted boldly at her, "Prepare to die, demon!"

The girl looked up at me with her eyes still full of tears as the demon was still lashing her. The demon charged towards me and I towards it. I plunged my sword into her, feeling kind of like a hero; however, I realized that I only grazed her shoulder, and I missed her heart. The demon just grew more and more angry and started fading into her body. Her whole demeanor changed. Her eyes became pitch black. I felt the atmosphere thicken with this evil presence. The demon and I were now standing face-to-face. It looked up at me and let out a loud screech. "Ba-e-e-e!"

The demon shoved me back by about ten feet. I heard a very low-pitched growl come from the girl. Her head was cocked to one side, her shoulders drooped, and her stance was widened. I look at her, very confused, but I charged again. I ran towards her with my sword held high above my head. I slashed downward with great force, but the girl did a front flip and jumped right over my head. She came back at me doing a roundhouse with her right leg and nailed me right in the head. I put my hands on my head, in an attempt to pacify the pain, but I decided to walk it off instead. This was not going to be as easy as I thought. The demon was relentless and let out another primal scream.

"Ba-e-e-e!"

It was like that one mosquito that you can't kill. I swung at the demon, and it exercised its great agility by dodging my sword's every attack. When I aimed for its legs, it jumped up and ran on the wall and then did an aerial over my head, like a parkour master. I was slashing away at the demon, but to no avail. I heard the honking sound of a car nearby. There were four guys cruising around in a 1959 Thunderbird. They looked like they just completed some 'recreational activities.'

"Whoa, du-u-ude," one of them said with smoke leaving his mouth as he spoke. "You see this?"

They looked over towards me. Another one tilted his sunglasses down, enough to where you could spot his bloodshot eyes. "Ma-a-an," he so astutely stated, as he and his friends pulled up to the same four-way stop that got us into this mess. *Man, this place is deserted if these guys are the only ones on the road.*

They stared at this battle between me and the demon in utter awe. Every time I swung my sword and every time the demon tried to attack me, I heard a chorus of, "Aw, man." Or I heard a "du-u-ude" as in, "Dude, this needs some theme music!" I continued to fight this demon, but upon hearing that, I dreaded hearing their selections to accompany this fight.

"I got this," the driver of the car said.

The Pokémon theme song begin to play. They were all nodding their heads in agreement. "Nah," one of them said, "this is a hardcore fight; so it needs hardcore music." The guy grabbed control of the mp3 player and pressed play. Harsh guitar riffs and mad double bass started to kick—August Burns Red.

This was getting very tiring, so I decided to try one more forceful strike. I drew my sword and made one final attempt at slashing her. I missed again, although I managed to catch her off-guard. I kicked her in the stomach, and then brought my sword around to slice her right down the middle. The demon finally left the girl's body and fell apart right in two. The girl was now just standing, immobilized by the shock of the events that had transpired. The demon now started to look like the Wicked Witch of the West from *The Wizard of Oz* and was melting.

I took one glimpse of this victorious sight. *Whew!* I then realized, *Oh, right. I have to plant a seed.* I put out my hands and tried to focus. I put my hands together, and a seed formed. It looked kind of like an avocado pit. I awkwardly moved the seed towards her chest, trying to avoid her breasts; and behold, a white, lotus-looking flower bloomed. The girl was now beginning to come to.

"What happened?" she asked, kind of dazed and confused. *Think quickly, Owen. Think quickly!* "Uh, nothing," I said calmly, making sure I didn't let her know how much I was absolutely panicking on the inside. "You OK?"

"Um…yeah," the girl said, no longer in a stupor.

An awkward silence then ensued.

"Well, I—" I began to mutter incoherently. I finally managed to get out, "Have a nice day!"

She walked back inside through the side door.

All right! I celebrated this private victory with a smile on my face. I turned around and I realized that the marijuana enthusiasts were still behind me.

"Dude, that was awesome!" one cheered.

"Woo-hoo!" chimed in another.

Their cheers and accolades were followed by applause, shortly followed by another honk. They had been sitting at the four-way stop for so long that other cars had begun to arrive behind them. They were now bringing the traffic around them to a screeching halt.

"Uh-oh," I said aloud.

"Do it again! Do it again!" they began chanting. But once again, it was followed by many honks because they were now clogging traffic.

I ran around to the front door to escape my unwanted audience. I noticed Marth walking out of the front door with the formerly very angry man. They were now together, and they were shaking hands.

And they're…laughing? What? I wanted to know what this was about.

"Have a good day, man." Marth smiled and laughed.

"I'm so very confused," I told Marth. "What just happened?"

"I'll tell you later." Marth sighed a rather victorious sigh.

Chapter Five

Marth and I walked back to the car like a couple of bad boys.

Bo-o-om!

I covered my head and jumped a little bit. I heard a very loud pop and saw a very large cloud of smoke. We looked quickly to the left and to the right. To the left and down the street a Laundromat was on fire. There were some cars on the road near the explosion, and they tried to take shelter in the fence surrounding the Laundromat. Cars were swerving off the road very quickly to avoid the explosion. I saw one crash into a stop sign. We decided to investigate the explosion. We were only a quarter of a mile away.

It was like a train wreck; you couldn't look away. We jumped in the car and drove down to the explosion site. We parked the car on the median and noticed that there was a woman running out and away from the Laundromat, which was now fully ablaze. Marth and I rushed out of the car and jogged closer to the scene.

"My father is trapped in there!" a woman screamed. She started running towards the burning Laundromat.

Marth held her back. "Ma'am, you can't go in there. There was an explosion, and now a fire is burning out of control," he said in an attempt to calm the woman down.

I noticed a man very close to the front door of the establishment. As he rolled out of the front door, he did so right in the nick of time, because the entire roof finally succumbed to the flames and caved in. However, he did not come out unscathed. His arm was on fire, and he was stopping, dropping, and rolling to extinguish the fire that was scorching his forearm. He was now starting to panic. Marth signaled to me, and we went over to see if the man needed any help. He had some small second-degree burns, but was otherwise OK. He was a white male in his forties with brown eyes, very fair hair, and a mustache. He had on a yellow shirt with khaki pants and dress shoes. We were sitting with the man on the other, safer side of the fence, away from the fire.

I looked up, ever so slightly above the man's head. I spotted a very sketchy-looking gentleman in the alleyway in between the now-incinerated Laundromat and the vegan burger joint next door. The man appeared to have some dark, shadowy wings.

I tried to get Marth's attention. "Hey, Marth!" I hesitantly moved my head up.

Noticing the guy, Marth helped the man to the sidewalk, and sat him down safely, while consoling his obviously concerned daughter. I took a good, hard look at this now-cremated Laundromat.

"Owen, you can handle it. Go!" he commanded. "I'll stay here."

I took off after this shadowy and suspicious figure. I was running towards him. He was aware of my pursuit; so he slid into the shadows back behind the alley. I continued my chase until I reached the alley. He turned the corner and disappeared into the dark depths of this rather dubious alleyway. The walls looked like they had seen better days. They were made of really rusty, red bricks, just barely held together with mortar, and coated with soot. There were dingy-green Dumpsters placed in a zigzag pattern against each wall and then one across from it. However, the alley had a dead end; and that dead end was enforced by another brick wall. I turned the corner as well, and saw the shady figure. The man looked over his shoulder, and noticed me following him. He darted away from me and my stare.

"Stop!" I shouted.

The stranger's face had one of those "Oh crap, I've been busted" looks, so he ran even faster. However, this did not frazzle me. I continued my pursuit; and I started to catch up to him. This guy was not having it. He stopped and he revealed some very grand, dragonlike, ebony wings. He began to run again and started taking flight. He was now ten feet off the ground and laughing.

Crap, I thought to myself, *that's a new trick.* I continued running after him. As my feet hit the pavement, I began to run faster and faster—and faster. I was booking it at like thirty miles an hour. My strides were becoming longer with each step. I touched the ground every ten feet. *Wow! Holy crap!*

The shadowy stranger dude seemed to be catching on, realizing he couldn't lose me. He turned back around and shot a dark, fiery ember from his fist. He aimed this shot, which was as big as a basketball, and it was coming straight for me. I freaked out for a second, and then I dodged it. *Phew!* It hit the ground and exploded.

Bo-o-om!

There was smoke and steam coming from the crater now beneath me. That didn't really look good. So the guy dished out another one of his fiery punches; and thankfully, I dodged another blow. I jumped so carelessly out of the way that I almost hit a Dumpster. There was a wire fence out in front of me. I just barely missed that one, too. I didn't know if I was going to make it. I closed my eyes and leapt, praying and hoping I wouldn't crash into the fence. I vaulted, almost taking flight, over the ten-foot fence. I twisted my body so that my back was facing the fence; and I glided over it, missing it within a couple of inches. I pulled my feet forward into a back flip, landed on my feet, and hit the ground running, amazed that I had just done that. The man was about twenty feet ahead of me and continued to shoot black fireballs at me. We were still moving deeper and deeper into the alley, both of us moving forward.

Suddenly, there was a shadow that appeared to be blocking the sun. Both the stranger and I looked up to the building on our left and were befuddled.

"Kiai!"

I heard a high-pitch shrieking and then *fwap*. I saw the shadowed figure fall; and his wings collapsed into him as he fell into the concrete. After he hit the ground, I saw a girl slowly float down. She was not short, nor was she tall; but she was wearing high-heeled boots. She had long, flowing, jet-black hair, held together in a ponytail. She wore skinny jeans and a loose-fitting T-shirt. I looked at her in awe and slight confusion. As I was still running full speed towards her, I realized then that I knew who she was. "Emiko?" I softly questioned.

I started having a flashback, in my mind's eye, of when we met in elementary school. I also realized that I was still running very fast, and that I did not have time for this flashback. I came back to reality as I smashed into the girl. We both crashed and fell into one of the disgusting, forest-green Dumpsters. The shadow man whom she had beaten into the concrete started getting up. After regaining his composure, he started laughing at us. He took off and got away. I sat up in the squalid Dumpster, in shock of what just happened, and in a little bit of pain.

The girl stood up and dusted herself off. "Watch where you're going!"

I stared at her, slack jawed, dazed, and confused. After a few moments of gazing at her, I blacked out.

I came to, eventually. When I woke up, I felt a stinging sensation in my face.

"Owen. Owen." Marth smacked my cheeks. "Wake up, wake up, wake up!"

I let out a groan and sat up. "Ow, my body hurts."

"Uh…yeah, because you were going about thirty miles an hour and you ran straight into a girl," Marth said so matter-of-factly.

I looked over and I saw the girl whom I collided with. I stared at her blankly for a few seconds. "Hey!" I said very dumbly.

Marth looked over at me with that "I told you so" face. "Yeah…smooth," he said, very sarcastically. Marth looked over at the girl. "I see you've already met Emiko."

Slightly irritated, I let out a sigh.

"Emiko, this is Owen."

We stared at each other for a few seconds as if we'd known each other for a lifetime. I could see her eyes widen. Her mouth was almost agape.

"Owen?" she said, very surprised. Then she said, very excitedly, "Oh, Owen! Hi-i-i!" She ran over towards me and hugged me very tightly. "Hi-i-i, Owen. It's me-e-e! You remember me?" She looked up at me.

I was excited and also very surprised, but I wanted to play it kind of cool. "So where have you been for the past ten years?" I asked her coyly.

"I moved back to Nagoya with my family and…well… became an exorcist," she said, very happily. "Now I'm back and I'm working here." She grinned from ear to ear. "I never thought that I'd run into you, chasing those kind of characters."

I appreciated her pun. "Uh, yeah," I managed, as I searched for words. "This was my first day on patrol."

"Wow! I see that you tapped into some of your abilities. That's impressive. Not many people do that on their first day."

I looked over at Marth, who made the OK sign and winked at me. I shifted gears. "So, what happened to that guy?" I asked nervously.

"Oh, he got away," Marth said, ever so nonchalantly.

"I'm sorry." I let out a dejected sigh.

"No, we'll find him," Marth said.

"Well, I'm going to start searching for him," Emiko chimed in.

"Uh-uh," I stammered. "Can I go with you?"

I could hear Marth snicker a little, then clear his throat. "I'm going to go report this and see if I can get any more information on these guys. I'll meet up with you later; but for now, see if you guys can figure out where he went. If you find him, bring him in," he said, going back to his serious face.

"How are we supposed to bring him in? I don't have any handcuffs," I reminded him, as I was still kind of a newbie.

"Emiko will show you how." Marth looked at me from the corner of his eye, smiling every second.

"This is going to be so much fun!" Emiko cheered. "I've never had a partner before."

We headed back into the street. My spidey senses started tingling; I cocked my head to the right. "I think we should go to the right. I just have a feeling."

"OK. I feel like he went that way too," Emiko said, less hyper.

So we started to walk that way, and I decided to have a little chat with Emiko. "So, are you going to school anywhere?" I asked sheepishly.

"Yeah, I'm going to Snow Creek High School."

"Oh! When'd you transfer?" I asked, kind of surprised.

"Um...yesterday. I just got all of my classes and everything." Emiko paused. "Yeah, I have ecology at ten o'clock," she continued, breaking the awkward silence.

"I have that class!" I said excitedly, like a dog wagging its tail. "I guess we'll be in the same class together." I chuckled a little bit to myself.

We continued our journey and wandered into an abandoned construction site. There were high beams, steel frames, cranes, and plenty of Keep Out signs. There were also small mountains of dirt, rocks, and machinery everywhere. We got to the start of the site and looked around.

"I feel like there is something here," Emiko said.

We were walking along the outside of the border and checking it out. We were about midway, when suddenly something popped through the fence behind us. It was furry and looked like a rhinoceros. It had tusks coming from near its mouth. It started to charge at me and mowed me over. It didn't stop charging. It continued, even through the fence. After it charged through the fence, it was still going.

Emiko helped me up. "Come on, let's follow it!"

"OK."

We headed towards the fence to jump over it. I put my hands on the metal and got ready to pull myself up. I heard a voice behind me say, "What'd I miss?"

Emiko yelped, "E-e-p!"

We both looked to see who it was. It was Marth.

She turned toward Marth and slapped him on the shoulder. "I told you to stop doing that," she said as if he had done that before.

"A demon just plowed me over and we're following it," I said.

"OK, get going then," Marth replied.

We jumped over the fence: Emiko first, me second, and then Marth. The creature was still running very fast. Right across the street was a church. The demon was still running and disappeared into it. The church had a tall tower and many broken stained glass windows. The church seemed to have had some fire damage, which made most of the building look black. It was sandwiched between two other rundown buildings that looked like they were in the same shape.

We were standing across the street directly in front of the church. There were no cars parked alongside the church or even in the adjacent parking lot. I noticed that there were parking meters, but they looked like they hadn't been used in a very long time and were just rusting away. The sidewalks were empty except for dirt and leaves. It was sundown, and it was getting quite dark out when out of the corner of my eye, I spotted the man. He was off to the side just chilling outside, smoking a cigarette.

"There he is!" I pointed him out to Emiko. "Should we bring him in?"

Emiko stopped. "Let's wait a sec."

We watched as he walked up some steps to the front door of the church. As he knocked, the door opened up and revealed three other men. They welcomed him in and shut the door.

"OK. Let's go," Emiko said.

"Wait!" Marth interrupted. "I need to make a call first."

Just as he said that, his phone started ringing. *Doo-doo-doo-doo.* "Hey," Marth answered. "Yeah, we are at the church and we found the guy. Can you get me some information? I'm kinda...still...uh...working, Actually, I'm out at this place. By any chance, are you at the front desk? Can you look something up for me?" He waited for an answer. "Great! Do you know anything about the abandoned church on Center Street?"

A few moments passed while we waited for a response.

Then the person on the other side finally found an answer.

"Uh-huh…uh-huh…hmm…OK. Thanks! Bye." Marth closed his phone and looked at us. "So, according to Jennifer, this building caught fire four years ago, and this whole area was stalled for construction because buildings kept burning down. They couldn't find the cause, so everyone just gave up on this place and took a loss. But… this church was leased, even in the shape it's in, ten months ago, to an R. Finster. We don't have any information on this person, but she's still digging." Marth put away his phone. "For now, let's go have a look."

We walked up to the church building. The stench of cigarette smoke filled the air around the church. Nobody was around; the streets were vacant. The streetlights were just now flickering on; just in time, too—it was starting to get darker. We were walking up the church steps and we pulled open the heavy cathedral door and walked in. We closed the door behind us. We saw the man that we followed here, and the guys who greeted him, up front in the pews.

There appeared to be a service going on, and a man dressed in priestly garb looked up and saw us. He stopped his sermon. "Well, come on in, Exorcists," he said very snidely.

There were columns holding the building up. Each column had a wall sconce with a lit candle in it. The building was dimly lit with many shadowy areas. There was a walkway right down the middle of the sanctuary with ten rows of pews to either side. There were thirteen people in the room, counting the four. They were spread out, each sitting in a different row of pews.

The priest slammed his book shut. "Service is over. I'll be seeing you all very soon." He squinted at us, seemingly sizing us all up.

The congregation glared at us as they walked out the door.

The priest let out a sigh. "Come in, come in. My name is

Randall Finster," he said as he welcomed us into the sanctuary. "Come in. Don't be shy, because the Lord is always with you, right?" he said, rather sinisterly. "He's always with you, right?"

Finster was very serpentlike. He had long, dark, greasy hair and his skin was almost translucent. He was very tall and slender and wore a black-and-white priestly habit.

"Yes, He is," said Marth.

"Well, well…, to what do I owe this pleasure?" he said sarcastically as he smiled sweetly. Then his smile quickly turned into a scowl. "What do you want?"

"Well, we mainly came in here to see a man we were chasing, but now we know who the brains of this operation is," Marth said indignantly.

"Operation?" Finster feigned innocence. "I don't know what you're talking about. There's no operation here, just divine appointments," explained the 'priest.' "And I use that term very loosely."

"Well…one of your followers just blew up a Laundromat and injured some people."

"Oh, no! That is terrible!" Finster said.

"Yes, and the gentleman who owned that Laundromat told me that he knew the man who blew up his shop. He also said that he had just left an organization he no longer agreed with and that this was his punishment for doing so," Marth said.

"I'll make sure that I talk to him." Finster smiled, snakelike.

"Well, we'd like to turn him into the police," Marth said, very authoritatively.

"Oh…um." He paused for a second. "I don't know who you're talking about, but I do have some friends who would be delighted to meet you."

The priest, if you could even call him that, snapped his fingers. Two demonic beasts came out of the shadows. One of them was giant, even humanoid. Its chest was like that of an ape, dark but hairless. His face was just as dark as his chest, except for his yellow eyes. The other one was a dark dragon. This one had a long, narrow neck, some black wings, a spiked tail, and talons that could rip through concrete. Both were very big, maybe fifteen feet tall, and they took up half of the church.

"These"—he lifted his hands, gesturing to the creatures behind him—"these are my friends. I've been learning how to tap into our commanding powers. These creatures will give me the power that I need to destroy all of you. So," he continued as he walked towards us, "there's nothing that you can really do about it! I know all about your rules and you cannot touch me because I have free will. I have free will to serve any lord that I want. I have the free will to bow down to any idol of my choosing. You people cannot touch me because it is my free will, my choice, to destroy all of you. You will all die soon. Now, get out!" He snapped his fingers again.

The demons got closer.

Filled with a righteous fury, I unsheathed my sword. As I did that, Emiko pulled out two daggers.

Marth put out his arms in an attempt to restrain us. He was looking down. "We'll go," he said, "but you know very well what happens when you play with fire. You get burned." He started walking out. Emiko and I followed.

I wasn't giving up so easily. "Come on, we can take him, man!" I shouted at Marth indignantly.

"No," Marth said firmly. He grabbed my arm in an attempt to hold me back.

I pushed his arm away. "Yeah, we can."

After that very brief tussle, I ran, with the intention of attacking the big ape demon.

Marth turned around and yelled, "Owen, don't!"

I charged him and sliced at him with my sword. The gorilla thing bared its teeth. He revealed his claws and swiped down at me with lightning speed. I made an attempt to slash him back, and I got slashed instead. I barely saw it coming. The force of the hit sent me spiraling back to where I started. I hit the ground hard and blood spat out of my mouth. I laid on the floor, already defeated. There were four slash marks on the left side of my ribcage that were about an inch thick, and blood was just oozing out of them.

I began to put pressure on the wound as I laid there, writhing in pain. Then I started screaming bloody murder. There were now massive holes in my jacket. I looked over and I could see both Emiko and Marth's eyes widen. Marth then unsheathed his two-handed sword. It was so grand that you could hear it. And in the blink of an eye, Marth sliced through the beast. He then cried out, with a sense of urgency in his voice, "Emiko, grab Owen. Let's go!"

"We will have our day of reckoning," Finster heatedly said. "This was just the beginning." He continued talking as he slowly moved toward us. "I didn't want to spoil the surprise, but your young Padawan learner over here just couldn't hold back. Now, he's spoiled everything. Oh, well. You'll find out in two days just how much power I will have. So long, all you Exorcists, because the world as you know it is about to change again. Now, get out!"

Marth was holding back the demons as Emiko came to help me up. She began to drag me out. Marth, still posing as a threat to the demons, wielded his sword and pointed it in their direction. He noticed us and quickly left his post and came to our aid. I was being dragged out through the door in immense pain, while keeping my eyes on Finster all the while. I saw him turn around, walk into the shadows, and vanish. They managed to get me across the street away from the Satanists' haven. They stopped and put me down on the sidewalk near a bench.

"Emiko, stay with Owen!" Marth ordered. "I'm going to get my car and we are going to go back to headquarters."

"OK," Emiko said, obediently and without question.

"Owen," Marth said, directing his attention towards me, "keep putting as much pressure on it as you can." Next, he faced Emiko. "Make sure he doesn't lose any more blood." He then set off in a sprint to retrieve his car.

Meanwhile, Emiko looked me over, clearly concerned. "Are you OK?"

At that point I had no filter. "No, I'm not OK," I snapped. "I got clawed by that freakin' gorilla-face thing." Still in pain, I took one really sharp breath, and let out a sigh. "Man, this stings!"

Emiko assessed my condition. "I've never seen anything like this...I've never seen a demon actually physically harm a human." She paused for a second. "This is new. I think this is what he meant. If he can get demons to physically hurt humans, the human race is in trouble. And if he can mount an army of it—"

In the distance, Marth's car approached our location. His tires screeched to a grinding halt as he slammed on his brakes. He hopped out of the car urgently.

"Let's get Owen in the car!"

Marth and Emiko assisted me into the front seat.

"Shotgun," I said with a whimper.

Neither of them acknowledged me. Once I was in the front seat, Emiko made her way to the back seat from the other side of the two-door car. Marth hopped in and we drove off in the direction of the Exorcist headquarters.

Chapter Six

I could feel how fast Marth was driving down the small dirt road. This road had rocks and pebbles; and Marth was speeding over all of them. I moaned with every turn he made and every corner we went around. Every single time, I was reminded of the pain that I was in. "I thought that demons couldn't hurt us in the physical world."

"Me neither. I have never seen anything like that before!" Marth exclaimed.

I could tell that Marth was truly surprised and in shock at the events that had just transpired. We were really hauling butt down the road. Marth clearly had no time for the city speed limit. I didn't see him look at his speedometer once all the way to the headquarters. Within a New York minute, we were there. We pulled up right in the front of the building. Emiko and Marth helped me out of the car. They each supported me under my arms and helped me to my feet. I made my way to the very front. I could tell that Marth was freaking out a little.

He opened the door for me as I trudged in, and Emiko followed.

I could see Jennifer still at the front desk. She only had eyes for Marth, so she perked up quite a bit. "Hey, Marth," she said cheerfully, whilst waving at him.

"Jennifer, we have to get Owen to the Healing Rooms," he said.

She turned off the bubbly excitement and almost without hesitating said, "I'll call the doctor." She picked up the phone on her desk and paged the doctor. "Dr. Van der Deck to the Healing Rooms. Stat," she said with a very urgent voice over the intercom.

We were all being led over to the other side of the building. Marth, Emiko, and I, escorted by Jennifer, walked through a double doorway. In the middle of the hallway, we saw a tall, bespectacled man with a bald head, blonde soul patch, and white coat. He looked like he was in his early thirties and had a tall, athletic runner build.

Jennifer stopped; so we all stopped. "Hello, Dr. Van der Deck," she said merrily.

He looked over at us, specifically Marth, and greeted us joyfully as well. "Oh, hey, Marth! It's nice to see you again. I haven't seen you in quite a long time."

"Oh, hey, Doc," Marth said. "We kind of ran into some trouble. This is my underling, Owen, and this is Emiko."

"Well, what seems to be the problem?"

"Um...well, my underling here jumped the gun, got slashed by a demon, and was harmed in the natural."

"Oh, wow." The doctor looked down at the wound. "I've never seen anything like this."

"Yeah, that's what I keep hearing," I interjected, with sarcasm dripping off every word.

The doctor cleared his throat. "Come into my office." He gestured to the door right next to him and opened it up for my entourage and me.

We all found seating.

"Owen, I need to run some tests on this," he said very factually. "So, are you OK? I see that you're bleeding. Before we do anything, I need to test your blood and tissues surrounding the wound."

The doctor pulled a machine right over to my affected ribcage. The machine had a telescoping arm with a camera lens at the end that he moved. He put it a couple of inches away from my side. He then sat down in his rolling, spinning office chair and rolled over to his computer. He typed in information on the computer and then some on the touch pad of the machine. "OK, Owen, don't move. I'm going to take a picture of this."

He snapped a shot of it and typed some more, and then a picture appeared on his screen. After that, he took out a cotton swab and swabbed a sample out of my wound. He checked it out and put it in a plastic bag. He then looked at my ribs again. "Wow, it really…it looks to be an inch deep, and it looks like the bone is scratched. That is remarkable."

"Yeah, yeah. real remarkable. I'm super stoked," I said.

Marth directed his gaze towards the doctor. "Hey, Doc, I'm going to go report this to the General."

"Yes, that's fine," the doctor responded, not even looking at Marth. He seemed to be entranced by my wound.

At this point, blood had stopped gushing out of me. For what reason, I didn't know. I looked over at Marth. "What's the matter? You leaving?"

"Yeah, but I'll be right back. Stay put…all right? The doc will take good care of you."

"OK." I did not question Marth. "Yeah, I can't really move around with this hole in my side," I added in an attempt to lighten the mood.

"Yeah." Marth walked out.

Emiko was sitting next to me now on the exam chair. "Don't

worry. It's going to be OK, Owen. You'll be all right," she said, trying to reassure me.

The doctor swiveled our way. "Okeydoke. I have all the stuff that I need right now. I just have to send it to the General real quick to let him know what's going on." He typed away on his keyboard. "And then we'll get you patched up."

I could hear the clicking of the keys as he typed.

Emiko looked over at my chest and stared at it intently like she was processing and scanning whatever possible information my ribs could give.

Then the doctor spun back towards me. "All right, you ready?"

"OK."

"Now"—he paused, trying to tactfully explain what he was going to do next—"you're going to feel a little heat on this." He touched my ribcage. "It's not going to be painful at all. You'll maybe experience a tingly sensation, but that's about it." He closed his eyes and placed his hands right above my injury, hovering ever so slightly over it. He looked like he was about to pinch it.

Dear God, I sure hope he doesn't do that.

He lifted up his right arm, and then his left. It felt like he was pulling stuff out, but it looked like he wasn't actually doing anything.

I was watching this and wondering what the heck he was doing. "What are you—"

Before I could finish, Emiko shushed me. "Sh. He's performing surgery on you right now."

I looked over at her, very bewildered at what she had just said. "He's not doing anything!"

"Yes, he is," she corrected me. "Just close your eyes and look."

"That makes absolutely zero sense."

"Just do it," she said, stopping me in my verbal tracks.

"Whatever." I closed my eyes and tried to tune everything out. I turned my head towards where the doctor was, and I looked down at my ribcage. I could see something. I saw the huge gash on my side getting sewn up with a needle by the doctor. I also saw this purple liquid oozing out of it as he was doing it. It was falling out and onto the floor. With each stitch the doctor made, more ooze fell out. Finally, he finished and zipped up. The once ginormous gash on my arm had now vanished. All that remained were three lines, three little scars.

"All righty, Owen. We're all done."

I opened my eyes and looked down at my arm. There was nothing there. "Wh-o-a," I began to stammer. "Wow, my ribs feel weird!"

The doctor rolled away over towards his computer.

"Van der Deck has been gifted with the power of healing." Emiko nodded. "He can fix anything—physical or spiritual."

Marth came back into the room. "Oh, Owen, is everything good?" he asked so nonchalantly about what I would call a miracle.

I looked up at Marth. "Yeah, all patched up." I showed off my ribs and its absence of blood and gore.

"Great, the General wants to see us now." Marth looked towards Dr. Van der Deck. "Is he all good to go, Doc?"

The doctor looked at Marth. "Yep, he's all good." He looked back over at me. "Have a nice day. Hopefully, I won't have to see you any time soon." Then his attention went back to the computer.

"Yeah, I hope so too."

Marth immediately left the exam room, followed by Emiko, and then me. Next, we made our way down the hall to the elevator. Marth pressed the number-five button, taking us up to the top floor. The ride was quick. We got out of the elevator, rounded a corner, and went left and then left again until we saw a set of double doors on our left-hand side. We walked through the doors and there was a sign on the door. It read General Hannon.

We walked into this room. It was a darker room than the others that we had been in. It was the most spacious room that we had been in—that's for sure. There was a solid cherry desk in the center of the room and a vast array of books on the bookshelves to the sides surrounding the desk. On the back wall, there was a mantelpiece with a navy uniform on it, a hat, and crisscrossed swords. Some model boats and airplanes graced his shelves. There were four chairs in front of this desk. There were a few light fixtures; and none of them were being utilized. There was a man, presumably the General, sitting behind the desk, using his computer. He was very muscular with broad shoulders, a black buzz cut, bushy, black eyebrows, and a very defined facial bone structure. He was wearing a white fleet admiral's uniform. "Welcome! Hey, Marth, welcome back!" He spotted us. "This must be Owen and Emiko."

"Yes, sir," Marth said, very concisely and without faltering.

"I've heard that some interesting stuff happened today."

"Yeah," I admitted, "it did."

Emiko stayed silent.

The General turned to me. "While you guys were making your way up here, I had a brief chat with the doctor. He told me everything, and sent me all the information about your chest. This is the first time that this has ever happened and been documented. I just wanted to let you guys know.

"This syndicate, the group of people that attacked you, is a group of satanic followers. We have never seen them as a threat. We've known about them for a while, and they have been under the radar—until now. We really don't have that much information on them. So what did you find during this encounter with them?"

"Well," I replied indignantly, "the main priest guy can control demons with one snap of his fingers. They're really big, and they can hurt us and rip our flesh off…stuff like that."

"All right then." He paused as he looked a little surprised too. "Did we acquire any information about them? Did we get a name? Did we get any idea of their plans?"

Emiko spoke up. "Well, he said that his name was Randall Finster and that something big was going to happen in two days. He also said that we'll find out and that the whole world is going to change."

"Hmm." The General rested his elbows on his desk and his fists underneath his chin pensively. "Two days? Is anything special going to happen in two days?" he asked himself before directing his attention back to us. "I'll have my guys research this and keep watch for any strange phenomena within the next two days. However"—he turned towards me—"I think that I have a hunch as to why the demons could hurt you, Owen.

"We believe that this man opened a portal to hell and that these demons were able to still receive the authority to have this much power in the natural. If they are in close proximity to one of these portals, the energy and the power coming from hell increases their power and they can do more harm. But I will have my men keep an eye on the place and see if they are up to anything; and I will relay any information that they acquired to Marth. He will let you know. I still want you guys in on this operation, if you are willing." He looked at me.

I didn't need to think for very long about this offer.

"Yes, sir," I answered. "Besides, I'd like to get some payback at these guys."

The General then looked back at Marth. "Keep an eye on these kids; we don't need any more casualties."

"Yes, sir."

"That is all. You are dismissed."

We exited the office in somewhat of a line, and made our way back to the front of the headquarters.

"Do you guys need a ride home?" Marth asked.

"Yeah," Emiko and I said, almost simultaneously.

We hopped back in the car and drove first to Emiko's house. Minutes down the road, we pulled up to a huge mansion. It was defended by a gate, security cameras, and guards. Behind the gate was a really spacious and lush yard with a long gravel driveway. The house itself was two stories and appeared to be very grandiose.

I was staring at the manor, and just taking it all in. "Wow!" was all that I could manage.

"I told you that my dad was a businessman, right?"

"Yeah, but you forgot to add the words wealthy or affluent in that description."

"Well...um...yeah. He does really well for himself. We're kind of billionaires. He owns multiple businesses and stock in many companies. Come over tomorrow. I'll give you a tour."

"OK."

"OK, I'll see you around eleven? Is that OK?"

"Yes, I'll be here."

She looked at me and smiled. "OK, I'll see you then." Emiko got out of the car and walked up to the guard at the gate. He let her in and she waved good-bye. "Thanks, Marth," she said sweetly.

We waved back. Marth and I drove away and headed to my house, which was about five minutes away. When we made it to my house, I got out and I thanked him. I watched as Marth drove off. I looked up at the sky to see a beautiful, starlit night. I touched my ribs where I once had scars, thinking back about the demon that struck me. "I guess this isn't a small world after all," I said into the atmosphere.

Chapter Seven

I awoke the next morning with excitement. Skateboard in hand, I walked up to the front gate of Emiko's house. I was stopped by one of their bulky could-probably-kick-my-butt bodyguards. "We've been expecting you," he said.

"OK." I was let in by the guard and walked all the way up the long driveway. I arrived at the front door. I was but a dwarf compared to this massive passageway. I very timidly knocked on the door. Within seconds, the door opened, and it was Emiko.

"Hi, Owen," she said excitedly. "Come in, come in, come in!" She let me in.

Scuttling my way in, I looked at her in awe; her beauty was breathtaking. I just wanted to stare at her—in a noncreepy fashion, of course. She was wearing a loose-fitting, white tank top with tiny, blue flowers on it and dark-blue jeans, accessorized with gold bracelets. Her hair seemed to be just straightened and was beautifully laid against her head. "Let me give you a tour!" she said, as her excitement continued.

"Great!" I didn't have too much time to think about my answer as she dragged me along, her enthusiasm increasing every step of the way. The house was massive. I'm not sure how many bedrooms and/or bathrooms there were. The theme of the house seemed to be oriental modern. Once you walked in the front door, there was a grand entryway. The ceilings were thirty foot high or more. To the left was a flight of stairs with cast iron railings leading to the second floor. Everything was white in this area: the walls, tile floor, ceiling, and steps. There were small trinkets that added splashes of color to the area. Most of them were placed in built-ins on the walls. We walked past the stairs, and up ahead on my left was a glass wall.

"This is our garden." She pointed to the giant glass case to our right. Behind it was an indoor oriental garden. It looked very neat and peaceful. There was a butterfly resting on a flower's petal while it softly swayed in the breeze. All the plants and grass were well kept and manicured; and they all got sun from the skylight above. The biggest feature was the rock fountain that spilled into the koi pond. There was even a little bridge that passed over the body of water.

"Cool," I said.

We continued walking and found ourselves in a big, open space. There, in the center of the room, was a formal living room area. There were two loveseat couches, five chairs, a coffee table, and a couple of high-top tables, all resting on a large carpet that took up most of the space.

"This is where we entertain guests when we have parties or throw benefits. And over behind the garden is the kitchen, but I will show you that later. Um…" She pointed to a hallway on the left side of the house. "Over there is the theater room and library. And upstairs we have my bedroom, my parents' bedroom, my dad's office, and a couple of guest rooms."

"Wow, this place is huge!" I was in awe, as I was so not

accustomed to this luxurious lifestyle. To my right were huge glass windows allowing in a lot of natural light. Past the windows, I could see a crystal-blue pool with a large, lush, green yard. This place had it all.

"What I really want to show you is where I spend most of my time." She grabbed my hand and we walked to the back of the house where, once again, giant double doors were. She pushed open the door and we walked in. I think my jaw dropped when I saw what it was. "This is our dojo." She smiled at me.

The room must have been the same size as the rest of the house. The ceilings were also the same height, which made the room look even bigger. The whole floor was padded with soft, colorful foam. There were three-by-three-foot squares, and it made a checkerboard pattern throughout the space. At the far end was an American ninja warrior course, complete with salmon ladder and warped wall. There was also a regular climbing wall, sparring area, and weights. To the left was the mother of all exorcist weapon arsenals. The left wall was filled with cases and stands stashed with weapons. A lot of them were mounted or hanging by hooks: staffs, swords, nunchakus, kamas, kunai knives, sais, and hammers—everything someone might need in a battle. Emiko started to take her shoes off and I followed her lead. I stepped on the mats and they had a springy gymnast-floor feel to them. I headed over to where all the weapons were.

My attention immediately went towards the weapons. I wanted to do something impressive. I walked towards the wall of weapons and picked up the biggest and most menacing-looking sword I could find. I took it out of its sheath. I began swinging it around. "Wa-a-ah! Kiai!" I let out, as I swung the sword to and fro around the training room, making it appear as if I knew what I was doing. *Swish!*

"I see you like the swords." A voice came from behind me.

It was Emiko.

"Yeah. I picked it up and I liked it."

"All right. I'm more into smaller blades and throwing knives—like this." She walked up next to me and plucked a kunai knife off the wall. She was assuming some kind of position. "Ichi! Kasai!" she yelled out.

A clay pigeon fired into the open area of the room and she threw the kunai knife. She nailed it, and the clay pigeon shattered and broke apart.

"Whoa, that's cool!"

She smiled. "You wanna give it a try?"

"Sure," I said, completely caught off-guard. "What do I do?"

"Stand in the center of the dojo and just ready yourself."

I walked over and prepared myself. "Kasai!"

One disc fired in my direction. It started slowing down, and it got close enough for me to cut it. I sliced through it with the sword.

"I wasn't expecting you to actually get it," Emiko admitted.

I looked up at her. "Gee, thanks," I said to her sarcastically.

"That was pretty impressive for a person that's never used a sword before. You're a quick learner."

"Oh, thank you," I said, feeling very flattered.

"Let's try something a little more difficult. Say, 'Yon! Kasai!'"

"Yon! Kasai!"

Four more clay pigeons were launched from the wall, but they were coming out in like slow motion. I looked at them quickly and then grasped my sword with both hands. I looked around and swung my blade up to the left. Quickly after, I slashed through the clay pigeon. I pivoted, and the sword sliced down through the other one. I then spun around towards the one coming from behind, and raised my sword and fragmented it in half. I looked out of the corner of my eye and saw that the last one was coming from my right. I drew my sword and shattered the last clay pigeon into pieces. It broke much quicker than the other ones. It was almost like the other ones were being broken very slowly.

My concentration on the task that I had just completed was broken. It was Emiko, clapping. She appeared to be very impressed. "Wow!" She rushed towards me. "That was really, really good." There was endless praise coming from her. "So what all has Marth taught you?" she asked, in a more serious tone.

"Um…um." I had to think about that for a minute. "Come to think of it…nothing really. Nope, not a darn thing. He's just like, 'Here's a sword, go for it.'"

"Well, there's much to learn. I've learned a lot over the years. Would you mind if I taught you a couple of things?"

"Not in the least," I said, genuinely interested in learning from Emiko.

"Well, we have a lot of different powers and, as you just noticed, we can slow stuff down in our mind and see things in slow motion. We also have a kind of super speed and strength. We can lift up as much as ten humans together sometimes. You just experienced the slow motion, I take it?"

"Uh-huh." I nodded in agreement.

"Hmm…you've already experienced the speed aspect; let's test your strength. In each thing that you learn, you can always improve with training. Let's go over to the weights." We walked over to where the weights were, and there was this massive weight currently on the bench press.

"Hey, Owen, try to pick this up." She pointed to the gargantuan weight.

"Hey!" I searched for words of how to feel. "That looks like it's four or five hundred pounds."

"Yes. Yes, it's five hundred pounds."

"I can't lift that!"

"No," she said so plainly, "not with your human strength.

You have to tap into that special inner strength that we were born and blessed with."

"All right." I passed her the sword and then cracked my neck a few times. I sat down on the bench. I scooted in and out until I was lying supinely on the bench part. I focused and put my arms out in an attempt to lift the weight. *Here goes... weightlifting attempt number one.* I grabbed the metal bar and tried to lift. Oh, snap! It was really heavy. I let out a moan and a strained cry. "OK, it's not budging!"

"OK, maybe not." She bent down and picked it up effortlessly with one arm.

I didn't know how to feel about this. "What?" I asked, dumbfounded.

"Yeah, see? It's easy." She smiled as she raised and lowered the humungous weight the same way one fist pumps at a rave. She did all of this with great ease.

"What?" I asked her, confused. Then I became indignant. "No. Sorry...She-Hulk!"

She put back the weight very daintily, with no difficulty. "See."

I let out a sigh. "Fine." I sat and then laid on the bench, focusing my energy towards lifting this weight.

I placed my arms up towards the bar. I breathed in, and then breathed out. *Weightlifting attempt number two.* I raised the bar up one inch. I celebrated for a split second. The weight got heavy again and my arms started to shake.

"No," Emiko interrupted. "Keep with the happy thoughts."

I maintained the bar's position and strained to do so. I started to remember what Marth told me in the training room: "It is what you make it. It's as light as a feather." I kept thinking to myself, *It's not heavy. It's not heavy.*

After a few seconds, I could feel the weight lessen. I was actually starting to believe that it wasn't heavy. It continued to get lighter. I took one glance at the weight above me and noticed that I was holding it as far away as my arms would reach. "Whoa, that was easier than I thought!" I decided to go all out and hold it one-handed. I let go with my left arm, and then I started pumping it effortlessly. It felt as light as a feather. "I am starting to like this."

"Yeah, it's very easy."

I decided that the weight couldn't handle any more of my flawless moves and machismo, so I put it back on the bar.

"When you were chasing that one guy in that alleyway, you experienced super speed. We can go even faster than that," Emiko informed me, her enthusiasm still soaring. "We can go very fast. Let me demonstrate." She knelt down on the ground. She then had just one knee on the ground. Her fingers and toes were also there. Her head was pointed down, as well as her shoulders. She then raised her hips up just a little bit. "Ready?" Before I even said yes, she bolted to the other side of the gym, faster than a lightning bolt. "See, Owen?" she asked, showing off her achievement. "Now, you try."

"What?" I was again dumbfounded by these newfound possibilities. "Man, this is crazy!"

"Yeah, it's fun, too." Grinning, she zipped right back and was now right next to me. "Now you try," she said enthusiastically.

"Oh, boy," I said, with both excitement and reluctance. I assumed the same presprinting position and prepared myself mentally for hyperspeed. I'm not sure what happened in the space between; all I knew was that I was now on the other side of the gym. "Whoa, that's cool!"

I zoomed back and forth and all around the gym. I darted in every direction. "I like this!"

Emiko started accelerating towards me, and soon she was running parallel next to me. We zigzagged all around the gym.

"Also..." She spoke loudly, but it was too little, too late. "Also, we have the ability to defy gravity!"

"No way!"

"Oh, yeah. Watch this!"

"We can fly?"

"Sort of. We can make ourselves lighter, basically. I'll demonstrate again." We both come to a screeching hault at the center of the gym. She put one knee on the ground. She pushed upward with one leg and jumped up to the ceiling. She was inches away from the ceiling; and the ceiling was a good twenty to thirty feet high. I looked up at her in amazement. She was floating back down. "You can even control how fast you're moving in the air. You can slowly descend or come back down rapidly."

"Hmm…" I tried to take all of it in.

She sped up and was back down on the ground. "It's your turn."

"All right. I'm still getting used to all of this crazy stuff." I jumped up and then subsequently fell down. "That didn't work."

"Remember: mind over matter."

"Ugh, this is ridiculous. OK." I jumped up, and for a second, I was inches off the ground. Suddenly, I was a foot off the ground, not floundering about, just floating. I began to move freely. "Well, this is interesting." I began to walk on the air, like one would walk on steps. "This is cool," I said, genuinely intrigued, as I freaked out on the inside. "Oh, my gosh! This is awesome!" I screamed as I flew up to the ceiling. I looked down to see how far I had come. "This is so cool!" I began to float down gently—back first. I noticed that I was still defying gravity, so I decided to do a couple of back flips on my way down. Then I gently touched the ground. "This is so-o-o cool!"

"Yeah, it's pretty cool. You're catching on really quick."

"What else can we do?"

"There's one more thing, and I'm not really good at it. But

I bet you are," she said, blushing a little. Then she got more serious. "We can create and animate different swords, armor, shields, and even weapons that don't exist. It's whatever you can imagine."

"Oh, cool! Show me!"

"OK. Um…I'm going to try to make small daggers." She put her hands out in front of her and closed her eyes. I saw a formless blob coming from her hands. Then it started to take shape and it smoothed out into a blade. The handles started to take form. She laid her hands out, like it was about to drop out into her hands. "Oh." She looked at her creation, genuinely surprised and impressed, I think. "I've only been able to do that a couple times." She looked at me. "Do you want to try?"

"Heck yeah! I don't know what I want to make though."

"Just think of something."

"OK." I closed my eyes and tried to focus. *Let's try an awesome helmet.* In just a few seconds, it started forming. It was a bronze-colored helmet with black trim and a white feather coming from the top. I opened my eyes and there it was. "Wow! That's so cool!" I turned around to show Emiko. "Isn't this so cool?"

"Yeah, very cool. I can't believe you did it. Yay! You're amazing! You're just a natural at everything, huh?"

"What else can we do?"

"I'm not sure. These are all of the things I know. My dad said that we'll learn things along the way; so there's still more things to come. Now, do you want to practice them?"

"I do."

"Great! Let's spar!"

"Wait! What?" I looked at her, incredulous. "Me and you?" I paused. "I've never really sparred against a girl before."

"So because I'm a girl, you don't want to spar against me?"

"No, no, no, no, no! Of course not." I again paused. "Um… well, would you look at the time." I couldn't even think of a way to finish that excuse. *Think of something quick!*

"Come on, I won't hurt you...that bad."

"OK."

"Pick up your weapon," she said, egging me on all the while.

"Wait! Won't we hurt each other?"

"No. I don't know the correct terms, but basically, our weapons can't harm other exorcists. They can only push them backwards. You can just think of it as friendly fire," she explained.

I was kind of impressed that she used a gamer reference.

"Here!" She unexpectedly chucked a knife at my shoulder. The knife stuck into my shoulder; and the area around the impact began to glow yellow.

I looked at Emiko with a shocked and extremely confused face. "Why would you do that?"

"For a demonstration," she nonchalantly answered.

I pulled the knife out and checked out the impact point. I felt no pain, and there was no puncture or tear in my jacket where the knife hit. It only left behind a faded-yellow patch of light gently resting on my shoulder.

"OK," I said, shooting my eyes back up at Emiko.

"Let's go!" I threw the knife back at her like a fastball down home plate. It headed straight for her face.

She gracefully leaned leftward and out of the way, reached back with her right hand, and caught it by the handle. "Our Enemy isn't going to hold back, so neither will I!"

My heart sank, and it felt like I had just made a huge mistake challenging her.

"Kiai!" Emiko came at me, swinging.

CHAPTER EIGHT

After sparring, we both had our hands on our knees, panting and trying to catch our breath. While standing there still trying to get some oxygen to my lungs, Emiko looked up at me. "You're very strong for someone just starting to use their abilities."

I looked up at her and smiled.

"But you need to work on your form, technique, and precision."

My smile quickly turned into a frown. I heard a loud slam; and I saw the huge double doors behind us open up. A man entered. He was an Asian man, and he was rocking a designer suit. His jet-black hair was combed over to one side, but there was no gel. There was no facial hair protruding from his tanned skin.

"Oh, Dad." Emiko looked up at the gentleman. "You're home?"

"Ah, yes." He let out a hearty laugh. "Konnichiwa."

He directed his gaze towards me. "Who is this? A boyfriend?"

"Daddy!"

He let out another hearty laugh; he seemed to get a kick out of seeing his daughter flustered. "I'm just kidding," he said, stifling his laughter. "My name is Mr. Tachibana." He extended his hand.

Right then, I was not making a very good first impression. I stood up straight, putting the sword in the sheath on my back. I extended my hand to shake his hand.

"My name is Owen. I'm a friend of your daughter's. It's very nice to meet you." I laughed nervously.

"The pleasure is mine." He looked me over quickly. "An exorcist, I see."

"Yes, sir."

"For how long?"

"About two days."

"Oh," he said, surprised. "I saw some of your match while walking through the front door. I didn't want to interrupt you; so I just watched through the glass doors."

He turned to Emiko. "Well, your mother and I are heading out for dinner later. Would you two care to join us?"

At this point, Emiko was very embarrassed, and her face was redder than any beet. "Daddy, is it OK if we just go out by ourselves?"

I perked my head up. "What? We were going to make plans for later tonight?"

Emiko faced me. "Would you like to go out?"

"Yes," I said—no questions asked.

She then turned back to her father. "Can I take him to one of your five-star restaurants?"

"I don't see why not. You two should go to the Blue Helm; it's my treat."

I realized that I was wearing jeans, a T-shirt, and a torn-up hoodie. I was in no condition to escort Emiko to a fancy restaurant. I raised my hand timidly and tried to catch everyone's attention. "Um…I don't really have anything that fancy to wear to such a classy restaurant."

"Not a problem." Mr. Tachibana laughed heartily yet again. "You look to be about the same size as me. You can borrow one of my suits. Emiko, why don't you take him to my wardrobe and help him pick out a nice suit. Owen," he said as I turned towards him, "if it fits you, you can have it."

Oh, my gosh! What just happened? "Thank you very much!" I responded, still stunned by his generosity. "You don't have to do that."

"No, no, no, it's fine. I have wa-a-ay too many suits, and I need to get rid of some. Anyway, I hope you two enjoy your night. I have to get ready for mine." He then locked eyes with me. "But I want her home at nine."

"Daddy!"

"OK, nine thirty." He smiled. We shook hands again, and he headed out of the room. "Bye-bye, you two. Stay out of trouble."

Emiko giggled. "We'll try!"

"Wow, your dad is really nice and very generous."

"Yeah, he enjoys blessing people when he can. He mainly does it for the surprised look on their face."

"I knew he did a lot of business stuff. I didn't know that he owned restaurants."

"Oh, yeah. We own like twenty. They're all really high-end, and we have franchises overseas in China, Japan, and Southeast Asia. We have a couple here in the United States."

Urghu. My stomach started to growl. I guess Emiko noticed because she turned and looked at me and then chuckled.

I also chuckled, though uneasily so. "All this talk about food made me hungry."

"I heard you're hungry. Let's go see what's in the fridge."

We walked to the other side of the training room, put up our weapons, and headed for the kitchen. Her kitchen was huge. It looked like my mom's dream kitchen with its high ceilings, granite counter tops, stainless-steel appliances, ginormous island, chef's refrigerator, and the works.

"Would you like a drink?" she asked politely.

"Um...root beer, I guess," I said hesitantly.

She went into the fridge and grabbed me a bottle of root beer.

"Thank you," I said shyly.

"Would you like a sandwich?"

"Sure."

"What do you want on it?"

"Turkey, American cheese, lettuce, and some Ranch."

She turned back to her fridge, gathered the ingredients, and prepared a sandwich for me. She then turned back around and handed me the sandwich. She proceeded to make one for herself and also grabbed a fruity drink and some snacks. We headed out the French doors onto the patio. It was the perfect day for this. The sun was out and there was a breeze.

We set up an umbrella, sat by the pool, and enjoyed our lunch. The pool was a shimmering cerulean. It had a waterfall that led to a smaller pool below. Her backyard was a huge, wide-open space. There were lush, green trees. The grass looked like it had been freshly mowed. The cement patio was decorated with chaise lounges, two daybeds, and an eight-chair table set with an umbrella protruding through the middle. We walked over to the table and sat down. We started munching on our sandwiches. There was one more thing about Emiko that I needed and wanted to know. "So...um...when did you get into this...um...exorcist thing?"

"Well, I started when I was twelve. It was a couple years after I left South Carolina. Yeah, it was really cool. My dad taught me a lot. He used to be an exorcist when I was younger. Now, he works with them in business ventures and invest-ments. I don't know about all of the things, but it's all very complicated."

"Oh, really? That's cool."

As we sat there talking to one another, hours just breezed by. I'd only been reunited with her for a couple of days, but it felt like I'd known her my whole life. As I looked at her face, I thought, *Wow, she is so beautiful! How did I even get here? Does she like me or does she just want to hang out with me because we're both exorcists? Either way, I'm excited to be here. But why would she ask me out to dinner if she didn't like me?*

The next thing I saw was Emiko's hand waving in front of my face. "Hello? Hello-o-o...Owen?"

I finally came to. "Yep...uh-huh...I was totally listening."

"What did I say?"

"Something about your dad?"

"Very believable. My dad does the same thing.

Well, it's about four o'clock. Do you want to get ready for dinner?"

"We just ate lunch."

"Well, yeah, but it takes me a little bit to get ready; and we have to find you a suit."

"OK."

After putting our dishes in the sink, we headed to the up-per level and made our way down the hallway to her parents' bedroom to find a suit. As we were wandering down the grand halls, we saw Mr. Tachibana in his study talking to someone on the phone. The entire office was see-through, and all of the walls were transparent. He was only separated by French doors. He looked over and noticed us through the glass walls and waved to us. We waved back. We walked further down the dark wood floors and on down to her parents' bedroom.

Their bedroom was huge and their closet was as big as my room. Their closet had a contemporary design. It was very neat and organized and had lots of space. Emiko's dad had tons of suits. Good Lord, it looked like there were one…two…three—two hundred or more suits!

"Wow, your dad wasn't joking about his suits. Does he have one for every day of the year?"

Emiko chuckled. "No, he doesn't have that many. But, that's a good idea."

"O-o-K," I said, like she was crazy.

"OK." She smiled. She fumbled through the suits and looked at them. "O-o-h, I like this one!" She pulled out this super slick, black sports coat. "Try this!"

I took off my hoodie and put on the jacket. "Wow! Perfect fit. This is nice."

"I like that one on you. It looks really good." She blushed.

"Yeah, I like it." I admired myself in the mirror. "How much is this worth?" I asked in jest.

"Oh, it's only five thousand US Dollars," she said, like it was no big deal.

Mouth agape, I asked, "Only?"

"What size pants are you?" she asked, completely changing gears.

"Um…thirty."

"OK. Try these. They're adjustable at the waist." She held them up to my waist and then matched my size. After pulling out socks, a white shirt, and a tie and putting them on the seating area, she stepped back and studied the outfit. "OK. I think it will look good on you." She handed me the clothes. "I'm going to pick out my dress. You can go change in the guest room; it's the second door down from here. After you're done changing, you can wait for me downstairs in the foyer."

"Where's that?"

"Down below us. And if you want, you can check out the theater room. I'll be a little bit, so make yourself comfortable."

I put on this highly expensive attire and admired myself

in the full-length mirror. Something about this suit gave me a sense of power and pride. I felt like a million bucks. The suit could not fit any better; it was perfect. I folded up my clothes and laid them on the guest bed. The bed was made up with bright-white sheets. Everything was white in the room except some gray pillows for accent.

I headed downstairs. I turned left into the loft, and in the middle of the mansion I saw three different doors underneath the stairs. Two of them were French doors and one was a regular door. I walked in through one set of French doors and I found myself in the theater room. Wow! There were eight movie theater chairs right square in the middle of the room. In one corner, there was a popcorn machine with a mini-fridge right next to it. In one of the middle chairs, there was a remote that was sitting on the center-most armrest. I sat down and got comfortable. I turned on the big television screen and watched some old nineties reruns. My phone buzzed, and it was my mom texting me.

Are you coming home for dinner?

No, I'm heading out to dinner with someone.

Who? Is she cute?

She's just a friend, Mom.

She?
Oh, my gosh!
You have a date and you didn't tell me. What's her name? Is she pretty? I want to meet her. Do I know her parents?

I'll be home later.

But I didn't get any pictures of you on your first date. You better bring her flowers! Now you be a perfect gentleman. Or I'll ground your butt until you have your Master's degree!

Bye, Mom!

Send pictures!

About half an hour went by. I looked at my phone for the time.

"Owen!" I heard a voice from afar. "Owen!"

Yep, that's her. I turned off the TV quickly and headed out the door of the movie room.

I saw Emiko walking down the grand spiraling staircase. Whoa! She was wearing this beautiful, sparkly, teal gown with aquamarine heels. Her hair was curled. She had makeup on and her skin looked flawless—not that there was anything wrong with it before. Her eyes really popped. She looked stunning. I just admired her, in awe of how beautiful and smoking hot she was.

Uh-oh. She sees me just blankly staring. Quickly, say words! "Asdfghjkl." *Oh, my gosh! That's not even a word.* "Whoa, you look beautiful!"

"Thank you." She blushed. "You look pretty handsome yourself."

"Um…do you mind if I get a picture of you?"

"Oh, OK."

"My mom texted me earlier and she kind of wants a picture of you, of us, and—"

"OK," she said excitedly.

I snapped a picture of her and then we took a selfie. I lifted my phone up to take the picture. I looked to see how the picture came out. I wasn't smiling.

"Owen, you should smile." She put her hand on my chest; my arm was around her. The phone was up and about to click when she said, "Smile."

I worked up a smile.

Once we were done with the snapshots, I asked her, "Ready to go?"

"Yeah."

"How are we getting there?"

"We can borrow one of my dad's cars or we can take my car."

"You have a car?"

"Oh, yeah!" She looked through her purse and pulled out a set of keys. We walked through a labyrinth of hallways and reached a side door, which I assumed led to the garage. Emiko flipped on the lights. I saw five vehicles that looked like they had just been taken off the showroom floor. They took up the entire room. Among the vehicles were an orange Lamborghini Aventador LP 700-4, a red Ferrari 458 Italia, a black Cadillac Escalade, and a pearl-white Audi R8.

"Whoa!"

Click-click. Bloop-bloop. The Audi's lights flickered.

"Yeah, my daddy got it for me for my sixteenth birthday," she said humbly.

"Oh, my gosh!"

"Do you want to drive it?"

"Yes!"

She handed me the keys and we walked over to the car. This was the best day ever. I went over to Emiko's side and opened the door for her.

"Oh, thank you. You're such a gentleman."

"Yes. My mom would kill me if I was not."

"What?"

"Never mind."

I closed the door and hopped into the driver's seat. I ran

my hands over the steering wheel. The interior was beautiful and spotless. *Oh, wow, this is a nice car!* "Also, how do we get there?"

She punched the address in the GPS without telling me where we were going. The garage door opened and we backed out of the driveway onto the road. It was exhilarating.

Vroom-vroom. When we got onto the road, I tested the acceleration and began weaving in and out of traffic. Riding in this car was like nothing I'd ever experienced. I thought the handling on my mom's minivan was nice... I think I cut five minutes off the time of arrival.

We finally arrived at our destination. There was a large roundabout with an overhang that accentuated the luxurious design. There were white posts out front, with a thick, heavy rope. The restaurant was a stand-alone building that was constructed on the side of a hill, right next to a lake. It had an upscale boathouse look to it. Just looking at it from the front, you would think it was a single story.

I stopped, and we got out of the car. Of course, I opened Emiko's door for her like a gentleman. I handed the valet the keys, and Emiko handed him a fifty-dollar tip.

"Thank you very much." The driver gave her a stub.

We headed inside. Once you walked in, the whole place opened up. It looked way bigger on the inside than on the outside. The multiple levels probably helped give it a more spacious, luxurious look. After a couple of steps in, you could see the exposed, white beams holding up the roof. It had a contemporary décor, circular tables, and white-and-blue wood throughout the railings. It reminded me of a cruise ship that I'd been on.

There were two men standing at the door behind a podium. They were both well dressed and clean-cut. They were staring at some papers in front of them. They both acknowledged us when we walked through the doors.

"Emiko! Great to see you again," one of them said with a thick Italian accent.

"It's nice to see you as well, Luca."

"I have the perfect table for you and your date." Luca motioned with his hand. "Come this way."

We followed him to the back of the restaurant where a table for two was set overlooking the water. The view alone was unbelievable. Through the window, we could see the waves gently crashing onto rocks twenty feet out from us. The sun was setting, and it just peered through the forest on the other side and shimmered off the sea. The water was constantly moving and making rhythmic crashing sounds ashore. The wooden deck off the back tied the whole view together.

There weren't many people around us and not that many in the restaurant. The closest people were an elderly couple fifty feet away. It felt like we had the place to ourselves. We took our seats and then Luca handed us the menu. "Now, shall I let you roam through the menu or…" He paused like he was waiting for Emiko to finish his sentence. And she did.

"Everything you make is so delicious; I wouldn't be able to decide. So I will be happy with anything you suggest."

Luca smiled and then looked over at me.

"I guess I'll do the same."

He beat on his chest and said theatrically, "Luca will not disappoint."

Seconds after he walked away, my phone started to buzz.

Emiko saw me check my pocket. "Who is it?"

I looked down at my phone. "It's Marth."

"Answer it!"

I picked up the phone. "Hello?"

"Hey, Owen. Sorry if I got you at a bad time, but I just wanted to ask you a question."

"OK."

"Well, the General sent some of our guys to stake out the

church, but there hasn't been any activity there. They finally went in and looked around and the place was empty. There was no trace of them or of them even having been there. So my question to you is: Do you have any clue as to where they may be?"

I thought for a second. "No."

"I didn't think so, but I just wanted to make sure. I just have a bad feeling about this right now. OK. I'll keep you updated if we find them. Bye."

I informed Emiko of the events that were happening, and she couldn't think of any place they would go either.

A few moments later, Luca arrived back at our table with the food, and it looked fantastic. "Please enjoy our pan-seared halibut with white asparagus risotto." He set our plates down in front of us, smiled, and walked away.

Emiko and I dove in. I took the first bite; the fish melted in my mouth. Oh, my gosh! I had never tasted something so delicious. I tried the risotto next; my face probably looked like I was about to cry. Everything tasted so wonderful—I couldn't stop eating. When I finished my last bite I looked over at Emiko. "Wow, my compliments to the chef!"

Emiko was still working on her meal. "Well, you can tell him when he comes back."

"Who...Luca? I thought he was just the waiter."

"No, Luca is the head chef here and basically runs the place. He said that he wanted to be the only person that cooks for me and my family."

"Wow! That's really nice."

"Yes."

My phone started to buzz. I reached inside my pocket and pulled it out. I looked down and saw that it was Marth again. I looked up at Emiko, concerned. I turned the phone towards her so that she could see who was on the phone.

"Answer it!"

I answered the phone.

"We found out where they are. Can you guys get to HQ now?" Marth asked with urgency in his voice.

I looked up at Emiko. "Yeah, we're on our way."

CHAPTER NINE

Emiko and I arrived at headquarters. It was still dark out, but the streetlights illuminated the parking lot. We parked the car and jumped out. Emiko headed to the back of the car, grabbed two backpacks from the trunk, and handed me one.

I held out my hand. "What's this for?"

"It's your clothes to change into. But not now. We have to go and get our orders first."

We started walking to the building and made our way to the elevator. Emiko led the way down the hall around the corner and into a conference room. The room was big, but nothing like the auditorium. There was a bunch of people in the room that I didn't know. I looked around and saw people talking and waiting for the meeting to start. We walked in and saw Marth standing over in the corner, talking to the General. We slowly walked over to him; it looked like they were just finishing their conversation.

The General nodded his head and smiled at us as he walked

away. He quickly glanced at our formal outfits. "Glad you could make it. Sorry if we ruined your evening plans."

I looked over and saw Emiko's face, which was slightly red. Three more people walked into the room.

The General stood at the front of the room. On the wall behind him was a huge screen with nothing displayed on it. "Now that everyone is here"—he cleared his throat—"there is a potential threat that is upon us. A man by the name of Randall Finster has been playing with dark forces and wants to make the world his. He is able to control demons and command them to do his bidding. He has also found a way to give demons dominion here. They can now harm us and make us fight with full strength. Mr. Finster gave us a warning that we'll find out in two days just how much power he has. I had the research team cross-reference anything special that was happening within these next forty-eight hours, and they came up with this..."

A map of a local mountain range showed up on the screen behind him.

"We have the first blood moon of this year. But for some bizarre reason, it will be straight above this mountain range. When a blood moon arrives, the spiritual atmosphere directly above is heightened. Our local Satan worshipers are heading to this position as we speak."

The General started to pace back and forth across the room while he was talking and then stopped. "We believe that Mr. Finster is trying to open a portal to hell."

People started talking amongst themselves.

"Quiet! Quiet!" he commanded. "Now, to our knowledge, this has never been attempted in our lifetime; but if he can do it, the world as we know it will be destroyed within the month."

"Let's not let this happen. OK?"

"Yes, sir!" everyone shouted simultaneously.

"I'm going to split you all up into three groups, and you'll each head to your assigned coordinates. You'll start there and fan out. Radio us if there is any trouble."

The General clicked a button on the remote that he pulled out of his pocket, and group names appeared on the screen. Everyone's attention was on the board as they hunted for their name and which groups they were in. I did the same. Marth, Emiko, and I were placed in Group C with two others.

Marth looked at Emiko and me. "You two, go get changed real quick. I'll go gather our team members."

We both ran to the bathrooms to change as quickly as we could. I opened up the bag and found a black army outfit. I thought it was going to be my clothes that I was wearing earlier. In the bag was a T-shirt, cargo pants, socks, and combat boots. All fit perfectly. I walked out and saw Emiko wearing the same thing.

"Well, this is embarrassing," I joked. "I gotta go change." I turned around and tried to make my way back into the bathroom.

Before I got one step in, Emiko grabbed my arm and started pulling me. "No! We don't have time." I guess she didn't appreciate my sense of humor.

We went back to find Marth. He was there waiting for us with two other people. One was a young, black male with an athletic build who looked to be the same age as me. He was wearing tight jeans, white-and-blue Nike shoes, and a form-fitting T-shirt. He also had three short lines shaved into the right side of his tightly cut Afro. The other group member was a beautiful, but strong-faced woman—the kind of face that could have a brick smashed up against it and it wouldn't leave a mark. She looked like she could be in her late twenties to early thirties. She had a short, jet-black hair cut in an asymmetrical style. She was wearing a brown bomber jacket, white shirt, jeans, combat boots, and leather bracelets on each arm.

Marth gestured to us. "This is Emiko and Owen."

We shook hands with them.

"Emiko and Owen, this is Tyler and Bridget; they will be working with us."

Tyler looked at me with big eyes and open mouth.

"I know you… I was there when you hit that one dude in the face with a cafeteria tray."

Emiko looked at me strangely.

I looked at his face and faintly remembered him sitting at that table.

Bridget interrupted. "Yeah, great kid. We gotta go."

We all headed to the bottom level of the structure and went into the parking garage where an army Jeep was waiting. Everyone hopped in. Bridget was in the driver's seat; Marth rode shotgun, and Emiko, Tyler, and I were in the back. We sped off to our destination.

CHAPTER TEN

The Jeep's engine roared as we flew down the empty street. Our vehicle was weaving in and out of the traffic, blowing past the other cars on the road. We continued along the highway until we reached our exit. We turned off onto our exit and followed the GPS to our destination. We could see the mountain from where we were as soon as we got off the exit. We headed towards it and found a neighborhood that was a couple hundred feet away from this giant slab of rock.

We turned into the neighborhood full of cookie-cutter houses. They all had some minor differences, but they basically looked the same. We continued following the GPS down to a dead-end street. The street looked like it had three more houses that were in the process of being built. The other five houses on the block were finished, and people seemed to have already moved in—just judging by the children's bikes on the lawn, pinwheels attached to their white picket fences, and the little garden gnomes placed across their yards. At the end of the cul-de-sac, there was a large forest. Bridget pulled up to the dead-end street and parked on the curb. Everyone got out of the vehicle. My attention was instantly directed to the smell of smoke.

"Is someone barbecuing this late?" Tyler asked.

Ignoring him, Emiko pointed to something in the forest. "Look!"

I could see a small flickering of light through the trees.

"Let's go check it out," Marth said.

We spread out and made our way through the trees. As we got closer, I could hear voices talking. I saw an open area ahead. It looked as if trees had been cut down, making a circle shape up against the mountainside. Finster and his followers were there, all dressed in black. They were performing some sort of ceremony around a large fire. We took cover behind trees so that we would not be seen.

Marth was the closest to the front. Emiko and I were on either side of him. Tyler and Bridget were back and to the left of us, but still in visual range. The fire was raging and formed a perfect circle. It appeared to be twenty feet in diameter. The people around the fire had now all joined hands and were swaying back and forth while chanting the same sentence over and over.

"What should we do?" I whispered to Marth.

"Let's radio the other teams and tell them that we found Finster," he said, in a hushed tone.

Bridget pulled out her phone and tried to send a message. She looked at it, lifted her head, and shook her head at us. Her phone said that the call failed. We all pulled out our phones and tried to make a call or send a message, but some sort of interference was not allowing us. I was guessing that we were on our own for the time being.

"OK. Let's stop this madness." Marth turned back and looked at everyone. "Get ready for battle just in case."

Emiko and I drew our weapons. My sword appeared on

my back as I reached for it. Emiko pulled two kunai knives out from a pouch on her thigh and wielded one in each hand. Bridget and Tyler didn't do anything, but their demeanor seemed to have completely changed. Marth got up and walked out right into plain sight. We all followed his lead.

Finster noticed us and silenced all of his followers with just a wave of his hands. "Ah, finally. I've been waiting for you," he said, in a very sinister tone.

"For what?" Marth yelled.

"For you all to witness my greatness. You probably know what my plan is; if not, you wouldn't be here."

We all stayed quiet.

"With the power of hell's army, I will rule this pathetic world; and you will all know my pain," Finster said with the intensity growing with every word. "This will be a great awakening for this planet. You *will not* stop me again! Now that the blood moon is directly overhead, we may begin."

"No! We're putting an end to this now." Marth started to walk over to Finster. As soon as he did, Finster's cronies broke off from the circle and lined up in front of him, making a protective wall around their leader.

"What are you going to do, Marth—hurt innocent people?" Finster asked snidely.

The people in front of us had blank stares on their faces. They were all are lined up shoulder to shoulder, so none of us was able to get by them. Then I started thinking of ways we could get by: jump over them, throw them out of the way, or cut through the forest. I'm sure Marth was doing the same.

Finster began to speak again. "Don't worry, Exorcists, because this is all *for the cause.*" It must have been a trigger word because all of his cronies' eyes went pitch black, and the person closest to the fire full-on sprinted into the flames. We were all stunned by what was happening. Upon seeing this, Marth tried to grab one person; but they did a spinning roundhouse kick at him and knocked him back a bit. One by one, they slammed themselves into the fire. Their screams of pain echoed through my head. Their bodies started to decay way faster than they should have. It took seconds for one body to completely disintegrate. It was like the life and soul was being sucked right out of them.

We all jumped into action to try to stop the rest. I got ahold of a man's arm; he looked at me with eyes that were as black as the night. He grabbed onto my arm, spun around, lifted me off the ground, and chucked me towards the trees.

Ughf! I hit the ground, losing all the air in my lungs. I shook it off. I felt like I'd been a ragdoll the last couple of days. By the time I lifted my head, I could see him make impact with the fire; and in seconds, he was gone.

I scoped out the rest of the team and everyone seemed to be in the same place I was—on the ground, defeated. All we could do was just watch as the followers gave up their lives. Their strength was unexpected. That surprised us, which gave them the upper hand. Our attention was now on their puppet master, Finster.

He was just standing there with a knife in his hand, holding it before his eye.

How can he be so calm after making that many people sacrifice their lives? He made my stomach turn. My anger was starting to rise up inside of me.

Finster arrogantly began to tell us the last bit of his plan. "All I have to do is one final thing. With one drop of my blood, I will open the gates of hell and control a power greater than any on this earth. I will destroy all that come against me."

Finster quickly slit his finger and flicked a droplet of blood into the air above the fire. I watched as it slowly fell, knowing that if it landed in the flames, the earth was doomed. I grabbed my sword and swung it around. I lunged towards the droplet with my blade, but it was too late. I was too far away;

and by the time my brain analyzed what I should do, the droplet was inches from kissing the flames. Still reaching for it, I saw the blood make contact with the fire. Boom! It exploded into a pillar of fire, shooting up into the sky. The shockwave from the explosion sent me flying back next to Tyler. I landed on the ground, the wind knocked out of me again. I whipped the dirt off my face and I got up.

"Well, this has gotten really heated," Tyler jested.

My ears were ringing; and I was trying to stay focused. I checked out the fire to see what had been done. The flames seemed to be consuming the ground below it. The earth started to crumble all around it. The flames sunk lower, like they were digging a tunnel downward. Then everything stopped. All but the sound of a cricket chirping and a gentle breeze blowing was heard. We all looked around like, that's it? We each stood up and dusted ourselves off. Then a shadow shot out of the hole. It flew around for a little bit in the night sky before landing right next to Finster.

It was the dragon from the church. Everything about it was more lifelike: the dark black scales up and down its body, the spikes and horns on its face, and the way it was breathing. This massive creature was the type that one reads about in Greek mythology.

"Welcome to a new era, Exorcists!" Finster shouted.

We heard some growls, scratches, and roars coming from the pit. Another flying demon soared out into the sky. Then a claw reached over the pit. Demons started climbing out of the hole and escaping from the underworld. We couldn't believe what had just happened. We were all ready for this war—so we thought…

Marth yelled to Emiko. "Go radio for backup!"

In a split second, I saw Emiko run back to the Jeep, climb into the driver's seat, and speed away. This was about to get very real, very fast.

Chapter Eleven

I couldn't believe it. I saw it with my own two eyes and yet I still couldn't believe it. This madman just opened a *portal to hell*! I had joined this organization just a few days prior, only to find myself facing one of the biggest threats they'd ever had. It was nuts! I couldn't stand by and just do nothing. I wanted to go down fighting rather than be named a coward for the rest of my life. So I had to get my head in the game and ready myself for this life-or-death situation.

"Mom, I guess I won't be home by 10:30."

I saw that a handful of demons had already made their way out of the portal. Some were flying overhead, and some were slithering or crawling around and knocking trees over. Some were the size of whales and some the size of rabbits. There was no color on them; they all seemed to be different shades of gray and black. They had a variety of fangs, horns, scales, fur, spikes, and tails—each one of them uniquely creepy in its own way. You could just feel the evil presence take over this area.

"Go! Destroy all you can see, and kill anyone who gets in your way!" Finster shouted.

All the demons at once let out a roar. Their faces all turned toward us and the houses behind. They started moving in the direction of the houses and spreading out.

"Move!" Marth yelled to everyone. It seemed like we were all in a daze, but his word seemingly snapped us back to reality. "Spread out! We can cover more ground that way." He raced toward a demon.

Everyone pulled out their weapons and armed themselves.

"Protect the houses and the people!" Bridget yelled.

Tyler and I turned our attention to the street with the houses. We could see people outside standing and watching. Tyler and I started running side by side to them. We shouted at a distance from them, "Run! Get everyone out! Quick!"

As we said that, a level-three demon that looked like a snake with wings and legs struck, apparently hoping to eat one of us with its giant head. We both jumped out of the way. Srursh! The concrete crushed under the immense power of the demon's attack. It lifted its head up to reveal a small crater.

I heard people screaming in terror from the houses. There were about twelve houses on this block and only eight were occupied. I saw a man standing outside his doorstep in his robe. I pointed at him and barked an order.

"You, go help! Get everyone out of here!"

He looked up at the demon, immobilized by fear.

"Go!" I yelled.

He jumped and started running toward the houses. He directed people out into their cars to get away safely. Once I didn't have to worry about people getting hurt, I could turn my attention to the real problem at hand—the snake thing that was going after Tyler.

I heard Tyler at a distance having a full-blown, one-way conversation with the demon. I heard him yelling:

"Why you coming after me? It's 'cause I'm black, right? Can't you find a nice little white couple to snack on? Why you guys always after the dark meat, man?" He started walking backwards with his hands up. "Whoa, whoa," he said to it, trying to calm it down.

The demon struck again. Tyler leapt up and was floating over its head. He extended his hand, palm opened, and a slender rod of light shot out with extreme velocity from his hand. The rod pinned the demon's head to the ground. Tyler then landed gently on the concrete.

"Whoa!" I shouted. I was kind of surprised that he did that.

The demon began to squirm. Its wings started beating, trying to pull itself out from underneath the rod. Tyler decided to jump on its back and impale it even more. He walked down its spine and shot thirteen more into it. It was now glowing with golden light rods that had been speared through its body. The demon became motionless and started to fade. Dark smoke poured out of each puncture hole and the demon slowly started to vanish. Soon after, the spears all disappeared as well.

Meanwhile, all that was left to evacuate was one man and a dog. The dog was a big boxer with brown-and-black fur. The man was trying to pull the dog away from the demons, but it looked like the animal wanted to be in the fight. Another demon emerged from the forest and started our way. The dog went ballistic and started barking even more. The demon's appearance resembled a gorilla, but with a slender figure and long, pointy ears. It was almost as tall as the trees in the forest that the demon had pushed down with great ease.

The demon ran at them, pounding the earth with each step. The owner of the dog was pulling on the dog to get it in the car; but the dog's collar broke, and it took off after the demon. Tyler ran over to hold the man back. I was trying to run after the dog, but it was too late. I heard a whimper from the dog and saw that the dog got caught by the demon. Without a second thought, the demon threw the dog up in the air and opened its mouth wide.

I heard a faint whistle through the wind. It was Marth slicing through the demon with such ferocious and speed. The neck of the monster pulled to the left, and then fell completely off. Its head hit the ground and dissipated on contact. Marth leapt up, snatched the dog out of the air, and landed right in front of the owner. He handed off the dog, and both dog and owner got in the car and left.

We could see in the distance that there were a few more demons climbing out of the hole. Emiko drove the Jeep back to where Tyler, Marth, and I were standing. She pulled up right beside us.

Bridget jumped down from one of the houses close by, sped over, and reported back. She made eye contact with Marth. "I managed to kill a couple, but more are climbing out."

Emiko climbed out of the Jeep. "I just got off the phone with the General and he said no reinforcements yet. Their ETA is one hour."

"We need a way to close the portal," Marth said.

"I bet I know someone who can help close it," I answered.

We all looked up at Finster. He was on the dragon, flying in the sky above. He landed on the side of a mountain cliff so that he could watch his plan in action.

Marth looked at me. "Owen, you're with me. We'll take out Finster. Everyone else, do what you can about these demons until reinforcements arrive."

Everyone spread out.

Marth and I headed towards the mountain where Finster was observing from. We ran with supernatural speed through the forest, up the cliff, and right next to Finster's side. He was close to the edge of the cliff, looking down at the chaos ensuing. His dragon was behind him, back a ways, but was keeping its eyes on us. We stood facing Finster. He looked over at us.

His facial expression remained unfazed.

This was a very flat, open area on the side of the mountain. There were a couple of boulders that were staggered here and there. A lot of loose sand rested on the ground, and it caused every footstep to kick up a little dust cloud.

"How do you like my army? They're quite ugly, but they will get the job done." Finster chuckled with a disgusting laugh. "With this power, I can crush entire cities, bring world leaders to their knees, and instill fear into anyone that crosses me." He paused and thought for a second. "And my parents never believed I'd do anything productive with my life. Oh, well."

Finster snapped his fingers. With tremendous speed, the dragon darted at Marth and pulled him off the side of the mountain; together they hit the ground below. I heard a thud, then roars coming from the beast. I don't think Marth was expecting that, because he didn't move an inch. I guess he was too focused on Finster.

Great! Now I'm left up top with creepy, I thought to myself. I stared at him, sword in hand. "Tell me how to close the portal!" I shouted.

"Ah, no," Finster replied. He stretched his arm out with an open palm. A black flame began to form; then he shot it at me. I moved to the left and slashed it backwards with my sword. He shot another one, and I did the same thing. I felt like he was just toying with me.

I ran in close to him to let him know that I was not playing around. I slashed at him; he dodged effortlessly—nothing but air. I swung my sword at him many times, not landing a hit. He had the same speed that I did. The multiple fireballs he shot at me all missed. We seemed to be fighting on par, so I thought...

In one motion, Finster spun down and used his right leg to sweep my feet out from under me, then landed on his right foot and used his left leg to do a back kick. He struck me with a powerful kick to my sternum, and I flew back a couple feet.

Finster stood up and looked at me. "You're just wasting your time. You can barely use your full power, and your skill level is that of a beginner. It's really sad. Why are you even fighting this battle?"

"Why did you kill all of your followers?" I said totally avoiding his question

"Kill them? No. They gave up their lives to help me usher in a new era."

"How could you make them do that? They're people! With families!"

"I didn't make them do anything; I might have given them a little push. Besides, it's all for the cause."

My anger continued to build up inside. I wanted to take his head clean off his shoulders. No holding back, I went at him with full force. "Ah!" I came out swinging wildly, slashing left and right trying to land a hit, but he continued to dodge my attacks. I backed him up to the mountainside where there were some free-standing boulders. I swung down and missed him. My sword got stuck in a huge rock.

Finster was about two feet from me. "What? Can't hit me?"

"No!" I swung at him one more time, but the rock I had my sword lodged in came with it. It felt as light as a feather. The boulder flew off my sword and smashed into the right side of Finster's body. The side of his head spewed blood. He looks over at me, touches his wound with his fingers and looks at the blood.

"And I was having fun." His face turned red.

I felt like I pissed off a temperamental serpent and was now going to pay the consequences.

Finster raised his hands up to his chest level and smoke came pouring out. The smoke combined to form two pillars on each side of him. The smoke began to take shape. It hardened and body parts were created. They formed some dark-skinned versions of himself.

The figures attacked me simultaneously, coming at me from both sides. I raised my sword in defense. They weren't as fast as Finster, but they were keeping up with me. I could watch their punches and kicks slowly come at me; but with eight different body parts coming at me with such power, I missed a few. They kept hammering away at me. I broke away from them and jumped onto the rock wall with my knees bent. I used my legs to spring out at them. I charged at one of the shadow clones with one hand on my sword.

Shing! I cut the clone from its left hip to its right shoulder. I tucked and rolled past them both and flipped back around quickly to analyze the damage I had inflicted. I saw that only a small bit of smoke was streaming out of the cut.

I needed to cut deeper if I was going to beat these guys. I really missed Marth right about now. This would have already been over if he had been here. The thoughts in my head roared on: *He's probably having as much fun as I am this second.*

The two clones came at me again. I jumped into the air in hopes of catching a breather, but no, they soared right above me, raised their foot, and struck me back down with the heels of their feet. The front of my body hit the ground hard. The sword fell out of my hands on impact and landed a few feet away.

Finster slowly made his way over to me. The clones landed on each side of me. My body ached as I tried to muster the strength to push myself up. When I tried pushing up, one of the clones stomped down on the middle of my back, pinning me down. I lifted my head to see what Finster was doing. I watched as he bent down and picked up my sword. He stood up, held the sword out away from him, and admired it. "What a nice blade, but"—he paused and took one really good look at my sword—"I think I could make it better."

He had an evil look in his eye. Holding my sword up in

the air with his right hand, smoke came raging out of his hand and surrounded the weapon. The smoke got tighter to it and attached. The blade got wider and morphed the shape of the sword into a black scimitar—a quite large one at that. The sword became solid and Finster spun it around to gloat. "Now I have a weapon in my possession that will cause even the heavens to bleed."

Finster came closer to me, and the clone retracted its foot from my back. I tried getting up again, but he kicked me like a soccer ball over to the edge of the cliff. I hit the dirt and slid a little bit until my head was almost over the side.

Finster looked over at one of the clones and nodded his head at him. It was the clone that I had sliced just minutes before, and he started to fade into a shadowy darkness. He melted down into a shadow on the ground and slithered over to me. He restrained my hands, feet, and hips with his shadowy form that was like a rope-sized layer laying up against my body. I tried to struggle, but it didn't budge. It felt like a two-ton anaconda was holding me down.

"You Exorcists are so annoying, always getting in my way wherever I go." Finster played with my sword. "I just want to chop you all up into itty-bitty pieces and feed you to my pets." He stopped and his face popped up like he just had a bright idea. "That sounds like a great idea." His eyes narrowed and he scowled at me. "Let's start with your arms." He stood right in front of me. Looking down, he glared at me with evil in his eyes. Some people think eyes are the windows to the soul. With this man, I saw no light, not even a glimpse of compassion. He raised the sword with one hand. He angled the blade toward my arms. He swung downward and…

Zappow! Lightning struck my forearms. My arms lit up with color. Finster was unfazed and continued with his descending slash. Did he even see it? But his blade made contact with my forearms, and it cracked. I looked up at my forearms, and I had two tattoos of swords, one on each arm. The span was from the pit of my elbow to my wrist. They both had the same handle, but one had a red blade that was as bright as a ruby, and one that was green, deep green, like an emerald. The detail was that of a skilled artist.

Finster stepped back, confused.

Both swords slid out of my arms into real bladed weapons; I looked up, amazed. I used all my upper body strength to slice through the shadows and cut myself free. I got up and I was ready for round two.

Finster raised his hands at the clones and they both split into two. Now I was fighting four of these things. They were all attacking me. They all got in a destroy type of assembly line order. The first one threw a roundhouse kick at me. I ducked, spun around, and cut him through his torso with the ruby blade in my left hand. The second clone tried a right jab, but I countered with my emerald sword to the back of his neck. The third came at me with a combination of punches and kicks, but I plunged both swords into his chest and pried the clone in half. I then walked through the dissipating smoke to encounter the forth clone. He reached out to try to grab ahold of me, but I cut through his arms and sliced him straight down the middle.

At that point, Finster must have seen me as more of a threat because he started shooting dark fireballs at me. I dodged, wove, and moved between them. None of them could hit me. He still had my tainted sword in his hand, and he rushed at me and swung. I caught it with both of my swords in a crisscross fashion. We pushed against each other, our blades touching, but Finster's side did not pull back. I pulled both of my swords apart and sliced his blade right off the handle. The broken piece of the weapon flung off to the side and stuck in the ground. I backed him into a rocky wall. He laid his hands at his side, dropped the handle, and stood against the dirt wall.

"How do we close the portal?" I yelled.

"You think you've won, boy, but you haven't! You only got this far because your God had to go and cheat."

"I think it's more like leveling the playing field. Now, how do we close the portal?" I said with a much calmer tone.

"You can't from this side; only from the other. Unless you want to give up your lives, there is nothing you can do." Finster chuckled evilly. He snapped his fingers, and I was easily distracted. I looked down at them.

At that moment, the dragon flew up and charged at me. I turned around to see this thing with its jaws wide open. I jumped out of the way as quick as I could. Finster jumped on the beast and they hovered in place out away from the cliff. Finster was standing straight up in the middle of its back. The dragon seemed to have cuts on it. I guess Marth was having a hard time with it if he couldn't kill it.

"Well, it looks like my time here is up. Good luck, Exorcist. Maybe you can show me some more of your tricks next time."

"What? Not going to stick around?" I shouted.

"No, I have other places to be, but we will see each other again. Good-bye, Owen Adler." He turned around and commanded the dragon to take off away from me.

I jumped up to try to get onto the dragon, but Finster shot a fireball at me to keep me away. I landed back on the cliffside, and all I could do was watch as he flew away.

Chapter Twelve

The dust stirred up from the winged beast was just starting to settle. I was enraged that Finster got away; but we had more pressing matters to attend to, like the horde of demons that were making their way out of hell. By looking down from the mountain cliff, I could see that there were only six demons still roaming around destroying things. There were more, but I believe the other exorcists took those demons out. I slid down the side of the mountain and gracefully landed at the bottom. I wanted to get back into the action and help out.

I saw Marth fending off a giant, lopsided jackrabbit, but Marth's right arm looked darker. As I got closer, I saw that his arm was burnt to a crisp from his hand up to his shoulder; yet he still swung his sword with ease and strength. He cut through the creature's belly; it fell to the ground and then dissipated.

Marth looked at me with glazed-over eyes. "We have to close the portal." He started to wobble a little. I went over to help him stand up straight. He put his arm around my neck, and I held him up.

"I know how we can do it. We have to close it from the other side."

Marth's breathing was getting heavier. I'm not sure if he understood what I said because all he did was reply with a grunt. His roasted arm was gushing blood, and his condition was getting worse by the second.

I've got to get him back out to the Jeep so he can sit.

His arm still around me, I helped him walk out of the forest to the Jeep. We made our way to the edge of the tree line and saw some headlights coming down the road. We continued making our way to the Jeep; and by the time we reached it, four Jeeps and three sports cars pulled up to us. About twenty people got out of the vehicles.

Everyone, except for three people, was dressed the same as I was, with black shirts, pants, and boots. The three individuals were wearing some cool-looking trench coats with the Exorcist insignia on them. One of them walked over to me as I was helping Marth into the passenger side of the Jeep. It looks like reinforcements had finally arrived.

"I'm Commander Roy of Region Six. My men and I are here to assist you in any way possible. Your general has updated us; and we are ready to fight."

"Great," Marth choked out.

Roy looked over and made eye contact with the other two officers. Roy then nodded his head at them and they nodded back. They started pointing and shouting out commands to the other exorcists. Most of them took off in different directions after demons; however, two other people stayed behind to set up an outpost with high-tech devices. I was not sure what they did, but they looked important.

Roy turned around to look at the giant hole in the ground. More trees had been smashed down due to the demons parading through that area. From where we were standing, there were only a couple of trees invading our vision of the portal. Another demon climbed out of the portal. This one had the appearance of a hairless Egyptian cat with long, apelike arms and a Minotaur body. We saw one of the newly arrived exorcists rush over to challenge it.

Roy stared at the hole, displeased. "So he finally did it. I thought he would have given up because of what happened to his family, but I guess that just fueled his fire." He paused and let out a sigh. "I wish I had seen this coming." He turned back to me. "The only way to close the portal is from the other side."

"That's what Randall told me before he got away, but I thought that he was probably lying."

"No, that information is correct. But we need the rest of your team here."

The other commander walked over, and she handed Roy an earpiece. Roy stuck it in his ear and began talking aloud. "All units, please have Marth's team report back here immediately. Over."

The other commander was a little shorter than me and had long, blonde hair that was pulled back into a pony tail. She stood with authoritative posture with both her hands behind her back. I couldn't tell her age, but she couldn't have been anywhere over thirty. Her flawless skin made her even more beautiful, but she still looked like she could go toe-to-toe with anyone here. The woman glanced at Marth and walked over to him. "Hello, my name is Rebecca. Your wound looks very bad and needs attention. I have been trained as a healer as well. Would you mind if I take a look at it?"

Marth just sat there. "Yes, please."

Rebecca didn't waste any time and started with the treatment. She raised her hands close to Marth's arm but didn't touch it. She moved her hands up and down his arm like she was using a sponge to cleanse the charred skin. As she was doing this, I could see some of the burnt skin return to normal. It took about three minutes to completely get rid of the charred skin. "You may feel a little dizzy from the dark energy being in you. You shouldn't do anything strenuous for a couple days."

Marth tested out his hand, arm, and shoulder, moving them all about. "That feels great. Thank you very much," he said in a sweet-toned voice.

Back where all of the other vehicles were parked, a pop-up tent with a table and radio were set up. This was probably how their communications were working. Roars of demons echoed through the area, accompanied by the sounds of clashing swords, pounding of the ground, and war cries from the battling exorcists. The larger demons were making the earth quake with each hit of the ground. Roy's troops were fighting the demons all around, but every minute that passed, another couple of demons climbed out of the portal. There seemed to be no end to this. We needed to close it—and fast!

I saw Tyler running from the tree line toward us. Emiko was following shortly after. They both reached the tent, breathing heavily and covered in dirt, cuts, and scrapes.

"Man, I must have taken out fifty of those suckers; and I ain't even made a dent," Tyler spouted out.

"I was near you the whole time and I only saw you kill three," Emiko informed him.

"Where's Bridget?" Roy asked.

"I haven't seen her since we split up, but she's probably still out there slaying demons," Tyler reported.

"So I guess it's just you three," Roy said.

Emiko and Tyler walked over and stood next to me in front of Roy, who spoke up. "We have to close the portal as soon as possible. Marth can no longer fight in his condition, so the burden of saving this town falls to you. Are you willing to take on this mission?

Tyler, Emiko, and I looked at each other. This was serious. We could all die if we went; but if we didn't, demons would continue to pour out of the portal and soon destroy our cities, states, and eventually the world. I figured we might as well bring the fight to them.

This is crazy. I joined a secret organization that has been protecting the earth for years from demonic activity. Then a few days after my recruitment, the entire world is threatened. I love my family; and if this will keep them safe, I'll do whatever it takes.

"How do we close it?" I asked.

Roy looked at me dead in the eyes. "With this."

He lifted his right hand up. He was holding something in between his thumb and pointer finger. I could barely make out what he was holding, but as I stared, I could tell what it was. It was a mustard seed. That tiny, circular seed was going to save the world.

"We're all gonna die!" Tyler shouted out.

Roy ignored him. "This seed is small, but it packs a punch. So once it's planted, get out of there."

"Will it explode?" Tyler asked.

"No, but it will close the portal quickly. So unless you want to get stuck down there, I suggest you get a move on. My men and I will take care of the demons that have escaped. You guys will have to drop down, plant the seed, and get out. I have no idea what could be waiting for you down there. The conditions will be extreme, so be careful. Emiko, I'm going to entrust you with the seed." Roy pulled a small test tube out of his jacket pocket and put the seed in it. He then handed it to Emiko who hesitantly took it from him. He turned to me and Tyler. "You two will be her bodyguards. Keep everything away from her while she plants the seed."

One of the exorcists that helped set up the tent and radio walked over to us. He gave the three of us earpieces, and we each stuck them in our ears. Roy then continued talking. "We'll stay in radio communication, so report back if anything goes wrong. Understood?"

"Yes, sir," all three of us chimed in.

I turned my head towards the pit. I heard a low rumbling coming from it. It got louder and louder. The earth started to shake a bit. High-pitched roars resonated from the portal. Everyone's attention turned in that direction. Something was rising from the hole. It took up most of the circumference of the hole. The creature squeezed its way out. It was the biggest demon that had protruded from the portal. It had all the features of a giant centipede, but with slimy skin and a scorpion stringer. Its hundreds of legs carried it out and smashed the forest area all around.

"Whoa! What is that thing?" Tyler shouted.

The demon let out another high-pitched roar. The front of its chest rose up and whipped its head forward. Something flew out of the beast's mouth. It spit a glob of something out of its mouth over eighty feet away. The glob landed on some nearby trees. The trees started smoking. As the glob dripped down, the trees began wilting and decaying.

"We can't let any more demons out of the portal. We have to move now. Let's go!" Roy took off running. It looked like he was going to take down this monstrosity of a demon.

Tyler and Emiko took off right after Roy did. I started to run, but my left arm was stuck. I looked back and saw Marth. He had a tight grip on me. He looked at me with a desperate face. "Stay safe, Owen."

"I will." After feeling his grip release, I took off to catch up to everyone. Marth was left standing by the Jeep and the outpost that had been set up. I fixed my eyes on the portal; and in seconds, I was there standing with Tyler and Emiko, our feet right on the edge, all hesitant about going down.

"Well-p, we're all going to hell." Tyler tried to lighten the mood. "Should we all hold hands or just jump?" Tyler asked sarcastically.

"Let's just jump," I replied.

"Great! You first." Tyler slapped me on the back. His slap caused me to lose my footing, and I stepped too close to the hole where the dirt wasn't sturdy. The ground under my foot caved, and I fell in backwards. I could see Tyler's facial expression, which was like, What did I just do? Oh, crap!

Emiko jumped in after me, then Tyler. "Sorry, bro!" he shouted as we were falling.

"I can't see anything," I said.

"I got this!" Tyler yelled back.

A light began to shine down from above me. It was one of Tyler's javelins. It was putting out a lot of light, and I could see everything around us. Tyler let out a groan. The light rocketed past Emiko and me and shot straight down. They just kept going and going. They hit the floor thousands of feet down. Tyler fired about ten more down and lit up the area below.

I could feel the temperature rise as the dry wind hit my face. *How are we going to land? Are we just going to hit the ground and die here?* The ground was quickly approaching and I was not sure what to do. Emiko grabbed my hand and we slowly started decreasing in speed. We landed gracefully on the ground and so did Tyler. All of Tyler's javelins were lighting up the area, and we had a good perimeter of sight.

"It's hot as hell down here, man." Tyler took a breath. "And oh, my gosh, it stinks down here! Oh, man…it smells like rotten eggs and doo-doo, bro!" Tyler said spastically.

Tyler was spot-on; it smelled terrible. I thought I was going to throw up any second.

"Actually," Emiko informed us, "it was overwhelmingly hot. A normal human would be incinerated instantaneously if they were in this heat; but since we were not, it just felt like 100 degrees to us."

"That's great," I said. "Could we hurry up?"

"Yes." Emiko bent down to the floor, pulled the seed out of the test tube, pushed it into the ground, and placed her hands over it to start the growth. We waited a couple of seconds and nothing happened.

"Why isn't it working?" I asked.

"I'm not sure," Emiko replied. "It should be growing by now."

I tapped on my earpiece. "Uh…Roy, we have a problem."

"What?"

"The seed isn't growing."

The radio went silent. We started to hear roars and screams from every direction. Tyler and I shifted into a low, wide stance, readying ourselves for battle. We moved out away from each other to scope out the space. Emiko stayed kneeling down right where she was, but looked around.

Marth's voice came through the earpiece. "All the earth is dead down there. You have to create a small patch of living earth to plant the seed. Emiko just focused on restoring the earth in one specific spot."

As I heard Marth telling Emiko what to do, a short demon walked into the lit area. It had two slim horns, pointy ears, and hands and feet bigger than its skeletonlike body. Spit was drooling down its fangs. I shot my swords out of each arm into my hand. The demon jumped up and tried to attack me. I swung at it with the ruby-bladed sword in my left hand and sliced it in half at the waist. Both halves fell to the ground. I looked at them. They weren't dissolving. The upper body half was still trying to move. I didn't kill it. Then I realized that when we killed demons on earth, they disintegrated and went back to hell; but we were already in hell. So that meant…

"Hey guys, we can't kill them here!" I shouted.

"Yeah, I noticed!" Tyler shouted back.

I looked over at Tyler, who was facing a two-headed demon

with long body parts. The head on the left had no eyes, but a long jaw like a crocodile that was slapped right on the shoulders. The one on the right had three eyes placed at the bottom of its humanoid face, with the mouth and chin on the top of the head. The figure was about three feet taller than Tyler and was using that to its advantage. Despite the three javelins stuck in its torso, the monster continued to swing at him with its long arms and knifelike claws. Tyler defended himself with another javelin in hand.

I saw a small, winged demon heading for Emiko. I grabbed the closest javelin to me and chucked it straight at the demon. The spear soared through the air and hit the creature in the chest, pinning it to the ground. I heard the sound of something hitting the floor behind me, and it was getting closer.

I looked over my shoulder and saw a beast jumping through the air at me. I spun around and swung both swords up at it, slicing its underbelly. Its paws missed me by an inch. I rolled as I struck, following the falling demon's trajectory. The demon was tigerlike with only brown, matted fur on the upper half, and it had three tails. At that point, I was sweating profusely. Then I saw eight more dark figures approach the light area. I knew I couldn't keep going.

"Are you done yet?" I yelled at Emiko.

No response.

Tyler and I were getting pushed back and were getting closer to Emiko. Demons were charging at me from the left, right, and front. I sliced and cut at anything that moved. *There's too many of them!* And I could see more demons flooding the area.

"Tyler, fall back!" I shouted.

"Coming!" he yelled.

Tyler started running back and began shooting the javelins a couple feet away from Emiko's back. Hundreds of javelins were flying from his hands. As he got closer, he curved them and shot them along her side. Tyler reached Emiko and began shooting the javelins behind him at the floor. I thought he was building a fence with them. He continued to spear them into the ground on his right and carried it on forward. I was running back to this newly built fortress. Tyler had left a two-foot opening for me to slide into. I rushed in and Tyler closed up the entry. He stuck his hands out like he was a puppet master and thrust the spears upward. All the javelins extended and grew. The upper area was now covered by this teepee of glowing spears.

We were safe—for the moment.

We were all tucked into the ten-by-ten space, surrounded by demons. They hammered away at the javelins; some quaked and bent under the attacks. Roars and screeches filled the air. Emiko was still concentrating on the ground. I looked down and I saw grass sprouting up.

Emiko opened her eyes. "I did it!"

Tyler and I gave her no time to celebrate. "Plant the seed!" we both screamed.

Emiko snapped out of her daze and reached for the seed. Demons continued to pound away at the spears. One was hitting really hard on the side next to me.

Thud! Thud! Thud! The demon smashed through the javelins, and shards of light went every direction. It looked me dead in the face. It was as if the Hulk and a water buffalo had had a baby. The demon's face was like that of a buffalo, and the body like that of the Hulk, except with reddish-brown skin. The demon tried to grab me through the small side it had knocked down. I sliced at its arms and cut it a few times, but that didn't bother it.

Emiko dropped down into the grassy area and pressed the seed against the ground.

The monster kept reaching for me. It punched more of the spears out of its way to open a space wide enough for it. It struck at me again; but Tyler shot some spears at its face, and they penetrated its head. It stopped for a moment like it was paralyzed.

Tyler dropped his guard and looked at it.

Uggff! The left hand of the demon swung at him and knocked him over to the side. Then he landed face-first on the floor. Most of the spears started to fade away. The darkness crept in.

I tried to see whether Emiko was successful at planting the seed, but I was slowly losing sight of her. Something jumped on me and tackled me to the ground. I could barely see my opponents now. I kicked it off me. "Emiko, hurry!" I yelled.

"I'm trying!"

Is this it? Am I going to die in hell?

"A-i-e-e-e!" I could faintly see Emiko next to three glowing javelins. A rather large demon was dragging her away from the grass area by her head. Without even giving it a second thought, I hopped up and ran full speed at the creature, swords in both hands. I leapt up and hacked off its arm. When I landed, I twisted around and cut off its feet right from underneath it. The demon cried out in pain and landed backwards. I threw the arm that was grabbing Emiko off to the side. I retracted my swords and scooped her up in my arms. I ran back over towards the green space.

Demons were slashing at me from each side. I was weaving in and out of them to reach the grass. We were feet from it; and I saw Tyler over close to it. Emiko was holding on tight to me. Her body was so light in my arms. The big Hulk demon was in front of me; and there were also demons to the left and right. I had no choice but to try to leap over it. I used all the leg strength I had left and pushed off the floor. I touched the demon's fist and pushed off, landing right next to the grass. I set Emiko down.

"Get us out of here!" Emiko knelt back down and resumed where she left off.

I saw Tyler ten feet away from us. I rushed over and grabbed him and quickly drug him over. Demons surrounded us. I laid Tyler right next to Emiko. He was completely knocked out.

I drew both swords out. "You want a fight? Come on!" I screamed at all the demons.

They all charged. I tried to slow everything down. I saw arms and claws all reaching and striking at me. I danced around Emiko and Tyler, keeping inches away from them. I swung my swords in every direction to keep these monsters away. Then I felt a hit to my back. This one came out of nowhere. A hot pain radiated all over my back. It felt as if I'd been branded. Another strike landed on my leg. A tiny, ratlike demon stuck its claws into me. When I looked down to see what it was, a strong fist hit my chest, knocking me over Tyler. As I was falling, I could see Emiko out of the corner of my eye. The seed was just now absorbing into the earth. Our mission was complete. Well, at least I would die knowing my family would be fine.

As I was falling backwards, I could see straight up through the portal into the night sky. A star sparkled at me. The star grew brighter and brighter. It looked like it was entering the atmosphere. The light was shining and it was right above me. *Is it going the hit me?* The golden light shot down with great force.

Boom! The impact was so great that it sent demons flying in every direction.

I looked up to see an angelic being. His face was inches away from mine. I could feel a rather large hand holding the back of my head. He caught me before I even hit the ground.

I looked over. In his right hand he had a spear, and it was stuck into the ground. I got up to get a better look. This angel was huge. He looked to be about sixteen feet tall. His wings were massive and they were decorated with rare gems. He was wearing golden armor. It looked like it was forged with the purest of gold. There was an opening in the front of his helmet and it revealed a very kind face.

The seed was planted and it started growing. Its branches began to reach up and grab at the sides of the portal as it began to close.

As the angel took all of us and flew up and out, I looked down from hundreds of feet up and saw the portal disappearing. We flew towards the outpost. Tyler's consciousness came back at the worst time because he freaked out and screamed, presumably due to the height we were at. The angel knelt down and set us gently on the ground. He smiled at me and vanished in the blink of an eye.

A full, white moon illuminated the dark night. Everyone's faces could be seen. The streetlights turned on, and then shortly thereafter, all of the lights in the surrounding area turned on; and it was good.

Tyler looked over at me. "Dude! We didn't die!"

He put out his fist for a fist bump and we bumped fists.

Then I felt arms reach around my neck and touch my chest. "Yay!" I heard Emiko cheer.

Marth and Roy walked over to us.

"Is anyone hurt?" Roy asked.

"No, just a little bruised and sore, but I think we will all manage," I replied.

"I'm just glad to see everyone's OK." Roy smiled.

"Yes, you all gave us quite a fright for a while there," Marth chimed in.

"I'm glad to see you are all well," Roy said, "and if you would excuse me, I need to get back to my team. We still have some demons on the loose." He turned around and walked off.

Marth spoke up. "Now I know you have only been with us for a short time, Owen, but I would like to offer you a job working with me. You've used skills that usually take other beginners months to learn. Your God-gifted talent can only be increased; and I can teach you so much more. You can—"

I raised my hand at Marth telling him to stop talking. "I'd love to."

"I know this may not have been what you signed up for, but you are now a part of this family."

I looked over to my right at Tyler. He smiled at me. I then looked down at Emiko, who had somehow managed to slip under my arms and was now resting her chin on my chest. Her face was dirty but beautiful, and she was smiling at me. "Let's celebrate while we can because tomorrow is a new day. Welcome to the Brotherhood, Owen."

Epilogue

A man in a hooded, black robe was talking to himself in the Edgefield cemetery. It was midafternoon and fall-colored leaves were everywhere.

"Owen, Owen, Owen, you should not have done that, getting in the way of my personal dream of world domination. Now, I have to take it to the next level. You've just made this personal, young Exorcist. I'll make sure that you won't want to fight this next battle. And you *will pay.*" He stops in front of a grave and stares at it.

The name on the grave was Michael Adler.